Praise for Laurel Remington's

"As heartwarming as a fresh cinnamon scone."
—*Kirkus Reviews*

"A well-paced, gentle, character-driven
story... Sweet and refreshing."
—*School Library Journal*

"A quick read with a lot of heart."
—*Bulletin of the Center for Children's Books*

CAKE AND CONFESSIONS

ALSO BY LAUREL REMINGTON

Secrets and Scones

LAUREL REMINGTON

sourcebooks
jabberwocky

Published by Sourcebooks Jabberwocky, an imprint of Sourcebooks, Inc.
P.O. Box 4410, Naperville, Illinois 60563-4410
(630) 961-3900
Fax: (630) 961-2168
sourcebooks.com

Originally published as *The Secret Cooking Club: Confetti & Cake* in 2017 in the United
Kingdom by Chicken House Ltd.

Library of Congress Cataloging-in-Publication Data

Names: Remington, Laurel, author.
Title: Cake and confessions / Laurel Remington.
Other titles: Confetti & cake
Description: Naperville, Illinois : Sourcebooks Jabberwocky, [2019] |
    Originally published: United Kingdom : Chicken House Ltd., 2017 as volume
    two of The Secret Cooking Club under the title, Confetti & Cake. |
    Summary: Twelve-year-old Scarlett's wildly successful blog may lead to a
    television show, the Secret Cooking Club has new members, and she is going
    to bake her mother's wedding cake, but trouble is looming.
Identifiers: LCCN 2018046515 | (trade pbk. : alk. paper)
Subjects: | CYAC: Clubs--Fiction. | Cooking--Fiction. | Baking--Fiction. |
    Weddings--Fiction. | Family life--Fiction. | Fame--Fiction. |
    Blogs--Fiction. | Middle schools--Fiction. | Schools--Fiction.
Classification: LCC PZ7.1.R462 Cak 2019 | DDC [Fic]--dc23
LC record available at https://lccn.loc.gov/2018046515

Source of Production: Berryville Graphics, Berryville, Virginia, United States
Date of Production: February 2019
Run Number: 5014250

Printed and bound in the United States of America.
BVG 10 9 8 7 6 5 4 3 2 1

CAKE AND CONFESSIONS

CHAPTER 1

The Bake-Off

IF I WEREN'T ALREADY FULL, I'd say I was in pastry heaven. Spread in front of me is a huge table covered with cakes—cupcakes, cakes baked in ice-cream cones, layer cakes, fondant fancies—all decorated with pastel-colored icing, sprinkles, chocolate shavings, gummies, and candied eggs. They're all so beautiful and different that it almost seems a shame to cut them to take a bite—just a tiny bite—of each one. But the principal is standing on the other side of the table with her camera, and she's counting on me to do this.

It's not easy, but I choose five batches to put on a "short list." I leave aside the cakes that look just a little *too* good—they might be store-bought, or maybe someone's mom helped them with the decorating. The ones I choose may not look the best, but they're the most creative. One batch of cupcakes is decorated with little nests made of red licorice, and I don't think it would be possible to fit another candied egg, marshmallow, sprinkle, or gummy on top. Brilliant! The next one is a chocolate cake with squiggly writing saying HAPPY EASTER, and a funny bunny made from goopy gel icing and decorated with Smarties and chocolate buttons. Then there are the ice-cream-cone cakes, a plate of cookies chock-full of glitter and decorations, a cake decorated like a spring garden—all different, and they all look amazing. Though I can barely eat another bite after sampling the cakes on the sixth-grade table, I can't wait to try these lovely things baked by the fifth graders.

The principal takes my photo as I cut a piece from each of them. I feel like I'm a real judge on TV's *The Great British Bake Off* as I take a bite of the chocolate cake. The sponge practically melts in my mouth. The icing is a little too sweet, maybe, but I don't mind. It's delicious.

In the end, I choose the cupcakes with the licorice nests. They're made from carrot cake that's soft and spicy, and the nests on top are too cute to resist. But everything about the cupcakes—from the time taken with the decoration to the taste—is special. These cakes were baked with love.

"I think these should win for the fifth graders," I say, smiling. "Do you want to try them?"

"Oh yes!" The principal tastes the winners—and all the others too—and nods. "I agree completely," she says. "Let's see whose they are."

She looks underneath the paper plate for the name. "Annabel Greene," she says.

I don't go to this school, so I don't know Annabel Greene, but even so, I can almost imagine that I do.

"That's perfect," the principal says. "She's new here and kind of quiet. This will really help bring her out of her shell."

"Good," I say. "She deserves this."

We choose the runners-up, and she ushers me into the auditorium to the assembly that's already begun. Another teacher is showing slides of a school in Malawi, which is the school's mission project.

"And some of these children have to walk seven or eight miles to school every day," the teacher is saying. "That is, when they're able to go at all. And if they break a pencil or lose a pen, there may not be another one. That's why every bit of money that we earn to help them buy stationery is so important. Your cakes are making a big difference."

Hearing that, I feel proud. Thanks to the *Secret Cooking*

Club, a blog I set up at the end of last year, five different schools nearby have done charity baking competitions. I've helped organize them—even though it's *such* hard work being a judge!

The teacher hands the microphone to the principal, who takes over. She explains about the charity bake-off—selling cakes after school to help raise money for the school charity. "And we're so fortunate to have a very special judge with us today," she says. "I'm very proud to introduce a talented young baker and blogger, and founder of the *Secret Cooking Club*. Please give a big round of applause for…Scarlett Cooper."

The second my name is called, my stomach churns with nerves. My knees feel weak as I walk to the front of the assembly. I love helping organize charity bake-offs, but I don't like drawing attention to myself. For two years before I started the *Secret Cooking Club*, my mom wrote a tell-all mommy blog starring the embarrassing details of my life. I felt like the whole world knew the moment when I farted at Christmas dinner or the smell of my gym clothes on a scale of one to ten. I became a hermit—no friends, no clubs, no interests. Anything to stay out of the limelight. Then I met Violet, a new girl at school who became my best friend. She and I started the Secret Cooking Club. And life hasn't been the same since.

My hand shakes a little as I take the microphone and breathe in. "Umm, thanks for having me here at your school." My voice always sounds strange coming through a microphone. "I just want to say that the cakes you've made were absolutely amazing, and I know you'll earn lots of money for the school in Malawi. I'm really lucky to have been a judge. So now, let me tell you who the winners are." I uncrumple the paper in my hand and read off the names. "For the sixth graders, the runner-up is Patrick Morgan, and the winner is Ayesha Hassan." I pause and wait as there's talking and clapping.

"And for the fifth graders, the runner-up is Grace Halliday, and the winner—and the overall star baker—is…" I pause for effect. "Annabel Greene!"

There's more clapping and a few whistles as the kids come up. I hand them each their prizes. A Secret Cooking Club badge and key chain for the winners, and for the star baker, a gift voucher donated by a local kitchen supply shop. Annabel Greene is a small girl with straight, black hair, who looks positively shell-shocked to be standing in front of everyone.

"Congratulations," I say to her, leaving the microphone aside. "Your cupcakes must have taken you ages to make. They were so creative and beautiful."

"Thank you so much." Her whole face lights up as she

smiles, and at that moment, my nerves are totally gone and I feel like I'm on top of the world. The Secret Cooking Club has transformed my life, and maybe it can transform the lives not only of children in Malawi, but kids right here at home.

"And now," I say back into the microphone, "let the charity cake sale begin!"

THE SECRET COOKING CLUB

April 15: Happy Easter!

It's been an amazing couple of weeks: a whole two weeks of no homework (and Mom not nagging me to do my homework), and lots of baking! Just a quick update on the Dubarry Hills School Bake-Off. It was fab-u-licious! The fifth and sixth graders raised more than $450 for a school in Malawi—how cool is that?! It was so fun being a judge and tasting all those delicious cakes.

Anyway, I'm off now—my best friend and I are going to make hot cross buns for Easter Sunday. It may sound old-fashioned, but we've got a fun new twist—instead of raisins, we're using dark chocolate. I've posted the recipe below. If you give it a try, make sure you share your photos!

The Little Cook

xx

CHAPTER 2

Hot Cross Buns

I REREAD WHAT I'VE WRITTEN, cross out "fab-u-licious" and type "great" instead. Then I delete that and put back "fab-u-licious." I hit post. Sometimes it strikes me as odd how different "The Little Cook" and I actually are. She's so confident and cool, and if I were reading the blog instead of writing it, I'd think she had the perfect life and want to be just like her. Which is great—don't get me wrong. It's just not really...me.

The doorbell rings downstairs. I put the computer to sleep and rush down to the door.

"Hi!" I say, flinging it open.

"Hey, stranger," Violet says. She pushes her shiny, black hair back from her face, and we hug each other.

"Sorry it's been a while," I say, feeling a little stab of

guilt. "I've just been so busy—with the charity bake-offs and the blog..." I stop. Of all the changes to my life that have come out of my starting the Secret Cooking Club—learning to cook (obviously!), fixing things with Mom (most of the time), and meeting loads of people in cyberspace through the blog and real people when we do events—by far the best thing is baking with my friends. And especially, having Violet as my best friend. I don't want her to think I don't have time for her.

"Never mind," she says. "I'm looking forward to making those hot cross buns! Are we going next door?"

"Yeah, let's."

We both go down the steps and scurry around the little hedge that separates my house from the one next door. I take the key from under the mat and unlock the door. The house used to belong to Rosemary Simpson, an old lady who taught Violet, me, and the other "founding" members of the Secret Cooking Club—Gretchen, Alison, and Nick—to cook. We used a special, handwritten recipe book she made for her daughter—the original Little Cook. Sadly, Mrs. Simpson died six months ago, and now the house belongs to her nephew, Congressman Emory Kruffs (also known—by me, anyway—as Em-K). Em-K has been dating Mom for a while now, and usually manages to be on hand to taste the latest free samples made by the Secret Cooking Club.

"I was thinking we could use chocolate chips instead of raisins," I say. "Em-K's coming over later, and he hates raisins."

"Okay, cool," Violet says. Though she's smiling, for some reason, she seems a little flat, as if something's bothering her.

I lead the way to the kitchen. From the outside of the house, you'd never imagine it was here. The whole back of the house is a huge kitchen, perfect for a cook, with all the gadgets, appliances, and space you could imagine. The cupboards are made of polished wood, and the work surfaces are shiny black granite. There's also a huge wall of cookbooks and a long table in the center that could seat a dozen people. On the fridge is a magnetic sign that we've left there out of respect—it says ROSEMARY'S KITCHEN. The kitchen is more than a great place to cook. There's a feeling about the place—a warmth, maybe—and not just from the huge stove in the corner. Sometimes when I'm here, I close my eyes and imagine all the delicious smells and tastes that have been created within these walls, as if I were there each time. It may sound ridiculous, but Rosemary's kitchen is the place where I feel happiest of all.

Treacle, Rosemary's black cat, jumps out of his basket by

the stove and begins to meow. He lives with us now, but he still likes to sleep here. I think our house is a bit too frantic for him most of the time, so he comes and goes as he likes through the cat flaps on the back doors of the two houses. I put down some food for him, and he swishes his tail and rubs against my leg.

Violet and I put on aprons—red with white polka dots—and wash our hands. She opens our special recipe book and flips to the page I've marked. Violet points to the drawing in the book of the little buns nestled together in a basket. "They look so cute," she says, "like little bunnies." She sighs. "I love Easter. Or…at least, I did when I was little."

I nod silently. Violet's parents were killed in a car accident a few years back. Now, she's living with her aunt Hilda. She doesn't talk about it much, but sometimes I catch her staring at nothing. I know she misses them and her old life, and I don't always know what to say to make things better.

"I used to like Easter too," I say after a moment. "My dad used to leave a trail of chocolate eggs and jelly beans all through the house that I'd have to follow to find my Easter basket…" I break off. *Dad.* I never think about him, and certainly never talk about him. I definitely don't want to start now.

Violet meets my eyes with a sideways glance. It's like we've both given up a secret without meaning to.

"Sounds nice," she says. "Now...how much chocolate do you think we should use?"

I think we're both grateful for the change of subject. We talk through the recipe, and I get out the flour, yeast, sugar, egg, spices, and butter, while Violet prepares the bowls, spoons, and baking trays. We start measuring the ingredients and putting them into the big ceramic bowl, and I put the milk on the stove to warm up.

Just as I'm about to start mixing, my phone chirps. I go and check it.

"It's Nick," I say. My stomach does a little flip. Nick Farr was the first boy member of the Secret Cooking Club, and lots of people at school think I'm his girlfriend. We have been out together—seen a couple of movies and a concert with his older brother. I've been bowling with his family and over for dinner a few times. We've been for walks where we've held hands and talked about random stuff. He has given me a couple of good-night kisses on the cheek. My insides still feel like pudding whenever I see him or think about him. But I've never heard him call me the *G* word. Sometimes, late at night when I'm lying in bed and can't sleep, I wonder if I've misinterpreted things between us. Or maybe I'm doing something wrong. I don't want to ask Mom, and right now, I don't want to ask Violet either.

"Is Lover Boy coming over to help?" Violet asks with a mischievous grin.

"Ha-ha," I say, reading the text. "No. He's off to his grandma's house."

"Shame," Violet says.

"It's fine." I pick up my wooden spoon, and we both start mixing, adding the warmed milk gradually and laughing as our spoons crash together. When the dough forms, we divide it in half and begin to knead on the floured kitchen surface.

"You're so lucky, Scarlett," she says as we work the wet dough.

"Me?" I look up, frowning. I know she's right, but lately, I'm getting a little bit sick of people reminding me of it.

"Yeah. I mean, your boyfriend is the cutest boy in the whole school! And things are good with your mom, right? And then you've got the *Secret Cooking Club* blog—I mean, you've already won a junior blogger award!"

I nod, not quite sure where this is going.

She gives me a little wink. "Not to mention getting to sample all those cakes at the charity bake-offs!"

"Hey." I pause, patting my stomach with a flour-covered hand. "It's hard work being a judge."

"I'm sure!" She laughs.

I laugh too, even though I don't really feel like it. On the outside, everyone thinks my life is happy and perfect, full of all-you-can-eat baked goods and delicious, healthy dinners. And if I were them, I'd probably think the same thing.

But there's one thing she said that really bothers me. She said "you"—talking about the blog—not "we." As I tackle the dough, I realize she's put her finger on another niggle, the little throb of guilt that I feel sometimes. I set up the blog as a cool online hub for kids who like to cook and bake. Plus, we were trying to raise money to help a charity for the elderly. I guess it has taken on a life of its own, but we're all involved with it. Nick and Alison help posting the photos, and Violet and Gretchen help with the recipes and answering the messages that come in. I'm the one who writes "The Little Cook" posts, but I've always thought of it as a group effort.

We tip the dough back in the bowl and cover it to rest.

"I mean, sometimes, I'd love to swap places with you," Violet says wistfully.

"But why? You're my best friend, and we're baking together, and we all pitch in with the *Secret Cooking Club* blog. And as for Nick, well, he's a good friend. But if he's any more than that…" I hesitate, "…you'd have to ask him because I sure don't know."

"Really?" she says. "I thought you two were solid."

"I don't know. It's…complicated." I haven't confided to Violet—or anyone else—my doubts about Nick and me, if there *is* a Nick and me, that is. "And anyway," I add, "you know that what things look like on the surface aren't always the truth."

"Yeah, I do." She sighs. I help her get the ingredients out to make the icing for the crosses. Whenever we bake together, I usually leave the decorating to her because she has a knack for making things look pretty. She measures out the icing sugar and sifts it into a bowl. She adds egg whites, a dash of vanilla, and a teaspoon of boiling water, and whisks the ingredients together.

But somehow, I'm not feeling quite as good as I was. As I watch Violet whisk the icing, I wait for the feeling of joy that I get watching the separate parts meld into one substance, impossible to separate, like they've always belonged that way. It doesn't come.

When the dough is rested, Violet and I knead it a second time. We fold and punch, fold and punch. It's tiring, but fun.

And then, from the other side of the wall, I hear voices and thunking bags. The wall that separates Rosemary's kitchen from our kitchen isn't very thick. I can tell it's Mom—she's been out shopping with my sister, Kelsie. "Help me bring in the rest of the stuff," I hear her say, sounding stressed and irritated.

"Mom's home." I keep my voice low, hoping I won't be asked to "babysit" my sister before we've finished. I punch the dough even harder.

Violet scans the recipe. "If we put them near the stove, they'll rise quickly. Then they'll need to bake for fifteen minutes. I'll ice them when they've cooled." She scoops the white glaze out of the bowl and into a piping bag. She also sets out two pots of edible glitter—pink and purple. Let's just say, with Violet doing the decorating, we go through a lot of edible glitter!

We both put more flour on our hands and start molding little balls, sticking them next to each other on a baking tray so they're almost touching. Then we cover the tray with a dish towel and leave the buns to rise.

"How are the two lovebirds?" Violet says. "Any word on when you'll be getting a new dad?" She cocks an eyebrow. "Emory Kruffs?"

"He'll never be my dad," I say, a little sharper than I mean to.

"Oops, sorry. I meant stepdad."

"It's okay," I say after a moment. Part of me wants to tell her all about my dad and why I don't like to talk about him and am glad he's out of my life. But I'm not sure I feel like putting it all into words. "It just sounded weird when you said it."

"The whole thing is kind of weird, isn't it?" Violet giggles.

"I mean, I just can't see him...I mean—or your mom..." The giggle turns into a full-on laugh. And I want to laugh too because I know what she means. Mom and Em-K do make an odd couple. I mean, he's a politician—a totally prim and proper upstanding member of the community. And Mom, well, she's anything but prim and proper—she's all over the place. But at the end of the day, they seem so happy together—which is what really matters.

Violet's laughter fades when I don't join in. "Sorry," she says again. "I guess I'm out of line."

Her purplish-blue eyes have a dark, bruised look about them now. For the first time, I realize it's not just today— actually, she's had that look a lot lately. I feel like I haven't been a very good friend. I pick up the baking tray and put it in the oven, slamming the door a little harder than necessary.

"Hey, come on." I go over to her and give her a quick hug. Her hair smells of sugar and apple shampoo. "Let's take a break, and I'll make some hot chocolate."

"Yes, please!" Instantly, she brightens, grabbing the milk from the fridge. I get out the cocoa powder, pausing to check on the hot cross buns, opening the cast-iron door a crack. Through the gap, I can see the dough rise and change shape as it bakes. I shut the oven quickly before the heat can escape.

How much easier things would be if I had a recipe for all the changes happening in my life—good and bad.

But since I don't, I settle for the next best thing—making a pot of frothy hot chocolate with miniature marshmallows, colored sprinkles, and a dusting of cinnamon on top—something that always seems to make life a little bit better.

· CHAPTER 3 ·

The Candidate

"SCARLETT, CAN I HAVE A word with you?"

Em-K rakes his black hair off his face, and, for a second, he looks like an overgrown schoolboy. His face and nose are kind of thin and longish, his eyes the same cornflower blue as his aunt Rosemary's were. When I first met him, I thought he looked somewhat stern—like a really strict old-fashioned schoolmaster who's just waiting to smack your hand with a ruler. Now I think he looks normal—and I like it when he smiles. But I still don't see what Mom sees. She and her friends giggle—actually giggle!—that he's very good-looking.

"'Course," I say. "Would you like a hot cross bun? Violet and I made them earlier."

Em-K came to check on his aunt's house just as Violet

and I had finished the last batch of hot cross buns and she was getting ready to go home. He found us in the kitchen, cleaning up. I remember the first time he found us there over six months ago. We were using his aunt's kitchen as the meeting place for the Secret Cooking Club when she was in hospital. He'd been super-angry at first—especially when we accidentally set the kitchen on fire.

Luckily, things have moved on since then. We're allowed to use Rosemary's kitchen as long as there's an adult around at my house—which is most of the time since Mom works at home.

"Do they have raisins?" he whispers behind his hand.

"We used dark chocolate instead."

"Ace!"

I smile at Em-K's attempt to sound cool. As he sits at the table, Treacle jumps on his lap and starts to purr. He strokes the cat's velvety fur, and I get him one of the hot cross buns. For a grown man and a politician, there are quite a lot of things that Em-K doesn't eat. Raisins being one, and nuts being another. I don't really mind—there are so many things out there to make, and practically endless ways to combine ingredients and put a new twist on old recipes. Not that I've got that much time right now to do that. But that's another story. And actually, Kelsie doesn't like raisins either, so it's no big deal.

"They're pretty," he says, smiling. "Very…uhh…pink."

I laugh. Earlier, after we finished our hot chocolate, the oven started beeping. Violet stood on one side of the oven, and I on the other, for what has become sort of a ritual between us. We each put a hand on the door and opened it together. It's one of my favorite parts of baking—the warm air escaping, hitting my face, bringing, in this case, the scent of cinnamon and warm, dark chocolate into my nose. The buns really looked like little bunnies nestled together, the dough light on the bottom and darker on top.

After the buns cooled, Violet started decorating. As well as putting a shiny glaze over the bun and piping the icing cross over them, she sprinkled pink and purple edible glitter and added a crystallized violet—a real flower covered with sugar—in the middle. They do look very "pink," but special too.

Em-K takes a bite. I watch his face as he tastes the different flavors. "Delicious!" he says. "I'll have another if there are any more."

"Sure," I say, pleased he likes them. "Would you like a coffee?"

"Love one!"

I make him a cup of coffee from the little espresso machine next to the sink. Em-K takes his coffee black with no sugar. I think that says something about him, though I'm not quite sure what. Dad always had his with half milk and three spoonfuls of sugar…

The coffee sloshes over the rim of the cup, burning my skin.

Dad? Where the heck did that thought come from? I never think about Dad, and now it's been twice in one day.

Wincing, I put the coffee on the table and run my hand under the cold tap. How do I even know how Dad—my father—takes his coffee? It's been almost five years since he left, and I wasn't exactly at an age where I thought about how adults took their coffee. I've seen him since, of course—he sometimes comes to town on whirlwind visits, and takes Kelsie and me out for dinner—I must have noticed his coffee then. Before I started the blog, the main contact we had with him was a card at Christmas and birthdays with five dollars stuck inside. Kelsie always begs Mom to take her to the dollar store or the supermarket to spend her money, whereas I've kept all of mine—shoved into a little ceramic fish piggy bank that came in a paint-your-own kit I got once for a birthday. I do the math—five years of Christmases and birthdays—I must have about fifty dollars. Maybe it's time I smash the piggy bank with a hammer, and get the money out once and for—

"You're not having anything?"

Em-K is staring at me. What is it with me lately?

"Um…Violet and I ate a couple that burnt around the edges. So, I'm not hungry." To make him feel better, I pour myself a glass of water.

"Won't you sit down?"

Something in the way he said that makes me pause. I place my glass of water on the table and sit.

He opens his mouth to speak, then closes it again like his tongue is tied in a knot. Sometimes if he's trying to make a point, Em-K will choose to be silent. But I've never seen him at a loss for words.

"I know we haven't known each other long, Scarlett," he says, his voice halting. "But these last few months have been the best of my life."

"Whoa!" I say. "Shouldn't you be telling this to Mom?"

He looks at me in surprise, then we both start to laugh. Treacle scrambles off Em-K's lap.

"Was it that bad?" he says.

"Awful!"

We laugh some more. I decide to have a hot cross bun after all.

"So?" I say, sitting back down at the table.

"I think you've guessed where I'm going with this, haven't you?" he says. He reaches across the table and takes my hand. I think about drawing it away, but decide to leave it. "I want to ask your mom if she'll marry me. But just so you know, I'm not going to do anything until I make sure it's okay with you."

"Like, you're asking me for my blessing, is that it?"

He smiles and gives my hand a squeeze, then withdraws it. "Yes. That's exactly what I'm doing."

I take a bite of still-warm hot cross bun and let the flavors of chocolate and spices melt on my tongue. "What if I say no?"

He sits up a tiny bit straighter. "I'm a politician, so I always try to please as many people as I can. But I know that I can't please everyone." He stares at the crumbs on his plate. I take pity on him and give him the other half of my bun. "So, if you say no," he continues, "then I guess I'll have to start a full-on campaign. Try to win you over. Unless there are any other candidates I should be worried about?"

"No." I grin. "I don't think so."

"And after tomorrow night, I'm hopeful I'll have one supporter at least." He reaches into his pocket and pulls out a light blue velvet box. "Look."

He opens the box. Nestled inside cream silk is a single diamond set in a silver-colored band. The stone catches the light and glints in a million rainbow colors. I can't take my eyes off the ring. He closes the box. "Will she like it?"

"I'd say we'd better start planning your victory party— isn't that what you call it?"

His face lights up. "So, I can count on your vote?"

I cross my arms. "There will be a few conditions to this... what do you call it...coalition? But hopefully we can work that all out."

"Wonderful! I'm sure we can!" He jumps up and tries to hug me. I put my hand in front of me.

"Starting with, no gushy hugs and stuff." I smile.

He sits back down. "No gushy hugs. Check." He draws with his finger in the air. "What else?"

· CHAPTER 4 ·

Spaghetti Bolognese

"SERIOUSLY, HE ACTUALLY ASKED FOR your blessing?" Violet gushes. "That's so…I don't know…weird!" It's Easter Sunday and Violet has come over to help me hide some eggs for Kelsie.

"Weird? I thought you were going to say 'nice.' Or—what's the word?—chivalrous."

"Sorry." She giggles. "It's just so Em-K. Is he going to do the whole down-on-one-knee-with-diamond-ring thing as well?"

"Yeah," I say. "We talked about where he should take her. I said he should take her to Bernini's—that new Italian restaurant. She loves Italian food…" I hesitate for a second. "And, it could be *their* place, you know? Somewhere she's never been with anyone else."

"You mean like your dad—"

"Yeah," I cut in. "That's what I mean."

I try to change the subject, talk about the returning to school on Tuesday, and about how I'm hoping we can bake a few more batches of hot cross buns tomorrow, and maybe some miniature strawberry tarts.

But Violet only wants to talk about the wedding. "You'll be a bridesmaid!" she says. "I'm so jealous—I've always wanted to be a bridesmaid. And Kelsie—I guess she's too old to be a flower girl. She can be a bridesmaid too. You can wear a fab dress and have your hair and nails done—maybe even go to a spa! And we can all help make the wedding cake. I'm sure your mom will have lots of people. We'll need like, six tiers with different flavors—"

"Six!" I say, feeling suddenly overwhelmed. "Come on. I mean, it's Mom's second time around. Does she really need a huge wedding with all those people? She had that when she married Dad—I've seen the photos. Maybe this time, it might be more romantic to keep things small?" It's like I'm pleading with Violet to agree with me. I'm so not into wearing fancy dresses and having to bother with things like my hair and nails. But it's more than that. I can't quite put my finger on it, but for some reason, the idea of Mom having a big wedding kind of scares me. All those people, and everything having to be perfect...

Violet rolls her eyes. "Small sounds boring," she says. "And from what I've seen, it doesn't sound much like your mom."

"Whatever." I shrug, not wanting to give Violet the satisfaction of knowing that she's absolutely right.

That night, I lie in bed, staring at the glow-in-the-dark stars on the ceiling. They were here when we moved into this house a few years ago, when Mom's blog started taking off. I suppose someone's dad—or maybe their mom—put them up years ago, maybe because they were into Star Wars or something.

In our old house, my room was painted pink with a Disney Princess wallpaper border that Dad put up when I was about four and completely obsessed with Ariel, Belle, Snow White, and Cinderella. He also used to come home from work just in time to put on the video, and I watched the princesses over and over again. Back then, I bought into the whole "ride-off-into-the-sunset-on-a-white-horse-get-married-and-live-happily-ever-after" thing. When did I stop believing in it?

Obviously, by the time Dad left Mom and they got divorced, I was over it. And for ages before that, I remember coming down before bed for a good-night kiss and finding them fighting.

As for Dad himself—I really don't think about him that much. He worked, he went to the gym, he came home, and he put on my video. Sometimes he'd watch the video with me, but mostly he'd disappear into his study and do his work or surf the internet on his phone. He spent most weekends with his friends, and otherwise, it was always just really Mom who was around all the time—yelling at me to do my homework and to put my dirty clothes in the wash. Taking me to the doctor to get cream for my eczema, pushing a screaming Kelsie in the shopping cart at the supermarket to stock up on fish sticks, ketchup, and frozen pizzas. Crying late at night because her marriage was falling apart and all her daughters could do was complain that the chocolate had all been eaten and Mom wouldn't let them play on her phone and all she did was yell and cry…

Spaghetti Bolognese. A sudden taste comes into my mouth. Tomato, oregano, and garlic. A long-forgotten memory. Sitting around a table—me, Kelsie, Mom, and Dad. It must have been a weekend. And something else. Dad—he was the one who cooked it. In fact, he even made the pasta fresh from scratch. It wasn't fancy or complicated, but it tasted good. And he was proud of it. Because he liked to cook but didn't usually have time…

The stars blur before my eyes. A tear has appeared from nowhere. Was that even a real memory? It must have been because I couldn't have just *made up* something like that about Dad. What else might I have forgotten?

Not that it matters. Instead of thinking about Dad, I think about Em-K—the best thing that's happened to our family for a long time. Sometimes it annoys me when he and Mom act all goofy and lovey together, but it's better than having them shouting at each other and someone leaving. The thing about Em-K is that he's like a rock—we can all lean on him and feel safe. And he and Mom love each other, that's the main thing. I picture the light blue box and his earnest face. Down on one knee at Bernini's, gazing up into Mom's gold-flecked green eyes; one by one, conversations stop and heads begin to turn. Mom's wearing a black jumpsuit that she bought on sale. She looks slim and elegant. Her unruly brown hair is held back from her face in a tortoiseshell clip I lent her.

And Mom—what is she thinking as the waiter brings over a chilled bottle of champagne? She'll say yes, of course, and everyone will clap. I hope she can appreciate the moment and how Em-K makes her happy. Happy in a way that her *Mindfulness for Moms* blog doesn't make her, her kids don't make her, her independence doesn't make her. Happy that for this moment, she's got the white horse (or at least a big, black Mercedes) and that she can finally call the builder in to start knocking out the wall between our house and the one next door, like they've joked about for ages.

Happy that for her, it's a new start—maybe for real this time. She can have the white dress, the bridesmaids, the wedding banquet, the honeymoon in the Canaries, and the new husband who was listed in *The Tribune* as number three of "Ten Politicians to Watch."

I close my eyes and turn over, blocking out the neon green of the stars by burying my face in my pillow. Because despite the list of "conditions" I gave Em-K, and the fact that I really am happy for both of them…

I'm kind of wondering where it all leaves me.

· CHAPTER 5 ·

Sushi and Canapés

I'M SITTING AT THE BIG table in Rosemary's kitchen. The room is warm and smells of freshly baked bread and slow-cooked roast. I pass a dish of herb-roasted potatoes down the table, feeling happier than I have for a long time. My whole family is here— chatting, bickering, laughing—just enjoying being together. Treacle is asleep in his basket. At the head of the table, Em-K carves the juicy roast, and at the other end, uncorking a bottle of wine is… My eyes widen. It can't be—

"Scarlett! Wake up!" Mom's voice jars me out of my dream. For a second, everything seems fuzzy, then my eyes adjust to rainbow sparkle.

"Look!" Mom says. She's flashing her hand in front of my eyes. "Isn't it beautiful? And from Tiffany's! I feel like Audrey Hepburn."

"Who?"

"Never mind." Mom doesn't miss a beat. "And it was the most romantic thing ever—a little Italian restaurant—amazing desserts!—and he even got down on one knee! Everyone was watching." She lowers her voice. "I didn't think Emory had it in him to plan something like that." She beams, fiddling with the ring. "But he did!"

"That's great, Mom," I croak sleepily, still clinging to the last threads of my dream. "I take it you said yes?"

"Of course! I mean, people were snapping us with their cell phones right and left. We'll probably be in the papers this morning." She smiles again. "In fact—I should go out now to the newsstand and have a look. Would you mind making breakfast?"

"No, that's fine." I rise on to my elbows.

She leans over and gives me a kiss. "Oh, Scarlett, I'm so happy. I love him so much! It's going to be such fun to be a real family, and I just feel that this time, it's right."

"That's great, Mom." I smile.

"But I was just wondering…" She lowers her voice. "I mean, do you feel okay about it?"

It strikes me how Em-K *must* be good for Mom if she too is asking my opinion. "You have my blessing, Mom. That's what I'm supposed to say, right?" I grin. "And I'm really happy for you." I hold open my arms to hug her.

"Thank you, darling." We embrace each other tightly. She's still Mom, and she still gets on my nerves a lot—I mean, she's always giving me "tips" on my blog and telling me that I can't cook with my friends until after I've done my homework. But I know that's just what moms do. And it's so much better than the days when she used to write stuff about me on her blog: how my room stank like a toxic waste dump, how she thought my best friend was dense, or how much being a mom made her wish she'd never had kids. Compared to those days, the little annoyances now seem like nothing.

She squeezes me so tightly that I can barely breathe, but this time, it's okay. I'm so glad to see her this happy and excited, and so glad that things between us are, for the most part, really good. Finally, we let go of each other.

"All right," she says with a hint of a frown. "But what about Kelsie? I mean—do you think she'll be okay too?"

"She'll get used to it." I shrug. Kelsie was very young when Dad left, so she has even fewer memories of him than I do. To her, he's like some kind of exciting character from one of her fairy tales, who is slaying dragons and rescuing princesses in a far-off land. I tried to set her straight once, but she looked at me with her big blue eyes, and it seemed like she was going to cry, so I decided she'd just have to figure things out for herself when she was older.

"I thought so too, but then…" Mom trails off, still not taking her eyes off her ring finger. "Never mind. She'll come around when we go shopping for my wedding dress."

She stares dreamily out of the window. "Part of me thinks we should just run away together—you know—elope. Me, Em-K, you and your sister, a few friends. Have a simple, romantic wedding on a sunny beach somewhere, with me wearing a summer dress and flip-flops." She smiles. "No blogging, no Twitter, and no stress."

"That sounds great, Mom." I smile with surprise and relief.

"But no!" She jumps up. "That wouldn't do at all. I'm marrying a congressman, after all. It will need to be the biggest, best wedding ever. I'll have an amazing dress, and you and Kelsie can be bridesmaids. Maybe I'll put you in pink… no…" she tuts, "…lavender."

So much for running away together—I knew that was too good to be true. I picture myself, itchy and hot in a puffy, lavender dress and dyed-to-match satin shoes that pinch. All those people, and photographers… My stomach lurches like I've gone over the top of a roller coaster. I want Mom to be happy, but it all just seems so *unnecessary*.

There is one thing, though, that might be good about Mom's wedding. The food. I've never been to a wedding before, but I've seen pictures of lovely tables laid out with all sorts of delicious, beautiful-looking food. Of course, it would be a huge job, but fun too. And I'm sure that with the Secret Cooking Club on board, we'd be up to it.

"Um, I was thinking maybe I could be in charge of the food instead of being a bridesmaid," I say. "Fancy dresses aren't really my thing."

I give a little laugh, expecting her to join in. But her lips are tightly pursed together, and she says nothing.

Propping up on my elbow, I turn toward her, alarmed by the sudden change. She's breathing in heavily, her shoulders rising like a piecrust ready to split in the oven. At first, I think she's doing some kind of meditation, but her face has that stressed-out look she gets when she has a deadline, or a meeting with a store chain, or someone leaves a bad comment on the blog, or some celebrity doesn't retweet her.

"You don't want to be a bridesmaid at my wedding?" Her voice has a sharp edge.

"It's not that," I say quickly. "And I really want to be involved." I smile reassuringly. "I'd love to make the wedding cake."

"The cake…" She ruffles the edge of the blanket absently.

"I haven't even thought about that yet. There's so much to do."
She sighs. "I'll need to get whole team of caterers, of course.
We'll do sushi and vol-au-vents for canapés, and then maybe
a four-course dinner. It will all have to be ordered special…"
She stands up.

"You…you don't want us to help?" I say.

She walks to the door as if she hasn't heard me. "Everything
needs to be perfect…" she muses. "I'm going to be the wife of
a congressman…"

It's all happening, I think the next day, as I get out of bed
and get ready for school. I'm happy for Mom, and more
importantly, glad that she's happy—for now at least. Because
she's already got a lot on her plate, and planning a wedding is
bound to cause more stress. And to be honest, I feel a little
hurt that she didn't take me up on my offer to do the food for
the wedding. I plan to look up exactly what vol-au-vents are,
because I don't have a clue. As I go downstairs to make sure
that Kelsie's ready for school, I think about the wedding cake.
Something tells me that Violet is absolutely right—if Mom lets
me try making it, it's going to need *at least* six tiers.

THE SECRET COOKING CLUB

April 18

OMG I have some mega-news. Mom is getting married! She's going to be Mrs. Kruffs. And guess what? I'm going to be making the wedding cake. It will be so amazing, but a bit nerve-racking too. Let's just say, I don't want to be the one who spoils her perfect day. So, I was thinking, six tiers, all different flavors—like chocolate and salted caramel, raspberry ripple, vanilla and lavender, red velvet—my mouth is watering just thinking about it, and I can't wait to start experimenting. And it will be covered with white glitter icing and a cascade of edible flowers. I'm not really the best at decorating, so I may need some help. If anyone has been to a wedding recently and has any suggestions, I'd love to hear them!

The Little Cook

xx

CHAPTER 6

The "Momster"

"I CAN'T BELIEVE SHE EVEN hesitated!" Violet sets down her fork, her mouth gaping in outrage. "I mean, anyone can have regular caterers, but not everyone can get a cake baked by the Secret Cooking Club."

It's our first day back at school, and we're sitting with Gretchen and Alison in the cafeteria. Today's lunch is baked potatoes with beans and cheese. Ever since we did the charity bake-off last year, the cafeteria ladies have been trying extra hard to improve the food. Baked potato day is one of the best of the month. The skin of the potato is crispy but not burnt, and the beans—well, no one gets everything right.

"It does sound totally bogus." Gretchen shakes her head. "But I saw your blog post—so she must have agreed in the end?"

I lean forward on my elbows. "She went downstairs this

morning and checked Twitter and Facebook. A few people tagged her and Em-K in some photos from the restaurant. She was all smiley and apologetic after that. She said that of course I should make the wedding cake. So, I decided to write her a nice blog post in return."

"Well, that's okay, then, I guess." Violet chews thoughtfully. "And what the heck are vol-au-vents?"

"I looked it up. It's finger food. Like a fancy name for sausage rolls."

Violet shovels in a mouthful of potato. "Can't see the point."

Alison laughs. Throughout my story, she's been strangely quiet.

"Is it really that funny?" I say indignantly.

"No," she says. "The whole thing is ridiculous. But completely normal, I think."

"That's normal? OMG—if that's true, I wouldn't want to be there if she started acting *not* normal!"

Alison takes a bite of broccoli sprinkled with cheese. "My sister got married a couple of years ago," she says. "I was a bridesmaid, and she used to bring over her wedding magazines so we could look at them together. It was fun…at first."

"At first?" Gretchen says.

She nods. "We were both like: 'that dress is so hideous'

or 'that cake is so OTT.' But then, I noticed she wasn't laughing anymore. Turns out she wanted those things after all. She accused me of spoiling her 'special day' and saying I was jealous. It was so bizarre. I was like, 'sorry—if you want all that stuff, then great, have it.' It was as if one moment she was my sister, and the next minute she was Bridezilla."

"Bridezilla!" Violet and I say at the same time.

"That's exactly what Mom was like," I say. "One second she was normal—she had this lovely idea of eloping to a sunny beach somewhere and getting married in a summer dress and flip-flops. The next second, it was sushi this and caterers that. And she wants to put me in lavender!" I wrinkle my nose.

"Yeah," Alison says. "That sounds about right. She'll want everything her way. And if it isn't perfect, then watch out."

"So when's this wedding anyway?" Gretchen asks.

"No idea. But as soon as possible, I hope. I'm not sure how long I can cope with a 'Momster' in the house."

We all laugh, and at the moment it is funny. We make plans to meet up after school and do some baking to bring to the old people's home like we do at least once a month. I use the last ten minutes of lunchtime to write a post on what we're planning to make—I'll post it later when I get home.

But as I'm walking home after school, my stomach begins

to knot. What will I find when I open the front door? Will it be Mom, or will it be the green-eyed, white-veiled monster?

I let myself in to the house. Kelsie is watching TV in the front room, so Mom must be home too. I put my bag down and go into the kitchen to make myself a snack. Mom's there talking to a big man in a checked shirt and jeans. He's got a measuring tape out and a clipboard.

"Oh, Scarlett, there you are," Mom says. "This is the builder. He's going to be knocking the two houses into one."

"Really?"

Mom looks at the builder and blushes. "I just got engaged," she tells him. "My fiancé owns the house next door. His aunt left it to him."

"Okay. So, do you want a doorway, or the whole wall coming down?"

"A doorway," I say at the same time Mom says: "The whole wall."

She looks at me, and for a second, I fear that she's about to morph into the "Momster."

"I just thought we could keep this room as a dining room," I say. "And leave Rosemary's kitchen as it is."

Mom's brow creases. Her eyes flick to our small kitchen table, which I notice is strewn with magazines. *Modern Bride*, *Country Bride*, *Vogue Brides*, *In-Style Bride*, *Perfect Wedding*, *Fantasy Honeymoons...* If this were happening to someone else, I'd laugh out loud.

Good thing I don't.

Mom sees me looking at her magazines and takes a protective step closer to them.

"Fine." She waves her hand like she's practiced making her ring catch the light. "Knock a hole through for now, and we'll go from there."

"Sure thing," the builder says. He checks his phone. "I can fit you in tomorrow morning."

Mom picks up her phone from the table and taps the screen. "Wednesday...hmm...I'm not sure..." She scrolls down. "Can you do it Thursday instead? I'm meeting a TV producer tomorrow."

They agree on a time and Mom walks the builder to the door. I open a tin on the counter and take out a caramel granola-and-seed bar that Alison made. She's really into trying to make healthy food that tastes good. This one's an experiment (because the first batch she made with just the seeds and granola was so bland). I put it on a plate and pour myself a glass of milk to go with it. I don't dare sit at the table because I might upset some kind of intricate filing system of bride magazines— with Mom, you never know. Instead, I stand at the counter and take a bite. This one is much better—the caramel adds just enough sweetness to make the bar taste good *and* healthy at the same time. I'm still chewing when Mom comes blustering back into the kitchen.

"Scarlett!" She enfolds me into a hug. "I've been waiting for you to come home. I so need your help. Sit down, will you?"

I plaster a smile on my face and reluctantly obey.

"I've been busy, as you can see." She flashes her ring hand again, indicating the magazines, and giggles. "It's going to be such fun, isn't it?" She moves *Modern Bride* to the side, and I see that underneath she's got half a dozen packs of different color Post-its. Her eyes are shiny as she hands me a single sheet of paper with a typed-on code:

> blue = cake
> pink = dress
> yellow = decorations
> orange = honeymoon
> white = food
> green = top tips

OMG. She hasn't even been engaged for twenty-four hours yet and already this is getting way out of control. My eyes snag on a handwritten note at the bottom. *Wedding Belles— Channel 3.* There's a scribbled name and next to it the word "producer." And a time—*Wednesday 2 p.m.*

"What was that about a TV producer?"

"Shh." Smiling, Mom puts a finger to her lips. "You have to swear to keep it a secret if I tell you, okay?"

"Um, sure." I don't point out that she's already told the builder.

"It's the *most* brilliant thing."

"What?" I say warily.

"A TV producer contacted me. She's a *huge* fan of the blog, and she's bought Mom Survival Kits from Superdrug for all her friends."

"Great…"

"She's doing a show about celebrity weddings, and she wants to feature me! Can you believe that—me, on TV!"

"Yeah, I can." I can totally see Mom on that show where people have to eat bugs in the jungle. Or maybe on *Dancing with the Stars*.

"It will be such a boost for my brand, you know. And secretly…" She leans in conspiratorially. "I've always wanted to be a real celebrity. This is my big chance."

"Wow, Mom, I didn't know you wanted to be on TV."

"Well, it will be exciting," she says, grinning from ear to ear. "And guess what else?"

"What? There's more?"

"She wants to feature you too. Isn't that amazing?"

"Oh." My heart does a dive. Mom may dream of being a celebrity, but I definitely don't.

"She *loves* the idea of you and your blog, and your secret club!"

"But if we're on TV, it will hardly be secret." I swallow hard, knowing that I'm grasping at straws. In real life, the club isn't "secret" anymore. I mean, we've posted lots of photos of ourselves on the website, and ever since our first online bake-off, word got out on social media that "The Little Cook" is some girl named Scarlett Cooper, and that her friends are Violet, Gretchen, Alison, and Nick. But in a way, that's been good—kids all over who want to join up can see that we're real people just like them. Our identities may not be secret, but there's a huge network of members out there, most of whom I'll never meet. And the fun thing is, sometimes when new people join up at our school, they leave cakes or desserts in the cafeteria at lunchtime, and we don't know who they are.

"Come on, Scarlett," Mom chides, sensing my lack of

enthusiasm. "You know how often we've talked about this. If you want your blog to work over the long term, you've got to keep it fresh—and keep getting exposure. Think of how many new members you'll get if you're on TV."

I nod reluctantly. It's true that Mom and I have talked a lot about blogging and online stuff—I mean, it's the one big thing we have in common. And even though it can be annoying to have Mom giving me tips on something that started out being a secret from her in the first place, when it comes to blogging and social media, Mom sure does know her stuff.

She's got thousands of followers who subscribe to her *Mindfulness for Moms* blog and meditation and lifestyle "Tips of the Day." She makes money from advertisers for things like exercise gear, vitamin supplements, and health foods. Not that it seems like she's been following her own tips—at least not lately. Mom's one of those people who thrives on stress.

"I know, Mom," I cave. "And I'm sure you're right—about the blog. But the thing is, there's a lot going on right now, and I want to be able to focus on helping out with the wedding." I point to the color-coded chart. "That is, if you want me to."

"Of course I do. But you shouldn't pass up this opportunity. It may all be happening at once, but we can make it work."

"Yeah, whatever." I sigh. It's Mom's special day, and I

was trying to go along with what she wants. But now that the wedding also means that I've got to be on TV…

Just thinking about it, my insides begin to knot up like in the old days before Mom's blog post was due to come out. Ever since then, I've hated the idea of drawing any kind of attention to myself. I know that lots of people out in cyberspace know my real name, but it's "The Little Cook" who's the real force behind the *Secret Cooking Club*. To me, that makes all the difference.

Mom switches on the kettle and sits at the table with her magazines spread before her. "Anyway, as far as the wedding goes, the TV station will help with the arrangements. They've got a team working on it. And, they're giving me a budget to spend. Still, there's just *so* much to do. Especially in two months."

"Two months?" I choke out the words. "Isn't that a little… um…soon?"

I remember saying to my friends that the sooner the wedding's over, the better. But this is just ridiculous.

"Look—it's their schedule, not mine. The show is filming next month. So, I'm thinking the wedding will be the end of June." She spreads her hands. "Besides, there's nothing nicer than a spring wedding. Though, I suppose technically it will be summer by then."

Two months. I take my plate to the sink and make Mom a cup of tea. Mom's already super busy, so how she's going to plan a wedding in that time, I have no idea. As I set the mug on the table, I glance at the pile of wedding magazines which has suddenly seemed to grow larger.

"I'm sure it will be amazing," I say. But Mom doesn't hear. Pushing the mug aside, she attacks the first magazine, armed with her rainbow of Post-its. I'm almost to the kitchen door when she calls out behind me.

"What do you think of these table decorations?" she says. "I like the peach flowers, but maybe pink would be better... or lavender."

Too late. Sighing inwardly, I accept my fate. I sit at the table, grab a pack of Post-its, and do my best to look interested.

THE SECRET COOKING CLUB

April 18

Here's another idea for spring. Today my branch of the Secret Cooking Club is doing our monthly bake for the local senior center. We're making their favorite—sticky toffee pudding—and then we're going to try something new: fresh lemon tarts. We're going to top them with raspberries, white chocolate shavings, and icing sugar. And don't forget the edible glitter—just a little! I think we all can use a little extra sparkle sometimes, don't you?

The Little Cook

xx

CHAPTER 7

Sticky Toffee

TWO HOURS LATER, I FINALLY manage to get away. My neck is tired from nodding: "Yes, I love that…yes, you'd look lovely in that color…yes, I think that's hideous too…yes, I think we could do that for the cake…yes, that would look good on TV." After about the first five minutes, I'd figured out that Mom and I have completely different taste. The wedding dresses I liked were sleek and simple, and my favorite wedding decorations, cakes, and food most definitely did *not* have pink as the main color. Or lavender. But it's Mom's special day, not mine, so while I tried to steer her away from the worst of the Disney Princess wedding stuff, I'm not sure how well I did.

By the time Mom left to go into her office to write a blog post that she was going to call "Plan Your Perfect Day," the pads of Post-its were practically used up, Bridezilla had thankfully not come out of hiding and, most importantly, Mom was happy.

I go out the front door and around the hedge to the house next door. I let myself in—I suppose it will be easier once the two houses are linked together, but I kind of like things the way they are. Mom has no reason to go to Mrs. Simpson's empty house, and Em-K still lives most of the time in his apartment. Don't get me wrong—it will be nice being able to use Rosemary's kitchen all the time. But I worry that it might be a little bit less…special.

I've already got a few texts from my friends wondering where I am. So I'm not surprised when I go into the kitchen and find them all there—Violet, Gretchen, Alison, a new girl named Naya, a new boy named Fraser, and…Nick. As soon as I see him, a flush creeps over my face.

"Hi," I say. "Sorry I'm late."

"No worries," Gretchen says. "How's the blushing bride?"

"She's great." I roll my eyes. "It's the rest of the world I worry about."

Treacle looks up from his basket where he's been asleep, blinks once, and goes back to sleep. I give him a pat on the head and grab an apron from the peg next to the fridge. It's our night to bake treats for one of the local old people's homes. We used to bake for them once every two weeks, but lately we've barely been managing once a month. I've already blogged that we're making sticky toffee pudding—hands down the favorite dish of the elderly residents (as one woman is fond of saying, "so sweet, and yet easy on the dentures")—and lemon tarts.

Violet is grating lemon zest for the tarts and, next to her, Fraser is pressing the pastry crust into little fluted tins. "Can I help?" I ask Violet. She lowers her eyes and nods. Once again, she doesn't seem her usual bubbly self.

"Sure," she says. "Can you measure out the sugar?"

"Yeah, um…" I look around for it.

"Fraser, can you pass me that bag of sugar?" Violet says.

"Um, what?" He turns his head from where he's been staring in the direction of Alison's blond ponytail, bobbing up and down as she and Nick are chatting and taking turns stirring the sticky toffee mixture that's melting on the stove top.

"The sugar."

"Oh…sure." He passes her an open bag from the counter.

Just then, Nick comes up behind me. He lifts his hand to brush a strand of hair off my cheek, and ends up leaving a thumbprint of flour. "Oops!" he says. My cheeks flush and even he looks a little pink.

"We thought you'd been bridesmaid-napped," he jokes.

"It felt like that," I say. When he turns to go back to the stove, I reach up to the spot on my cheek where he touched it.

Violet stops grating the lemon and looks at me. I take my hand away, feeling awkward.

"And it gets worse," I say, eager to fill the void. "She wants me to be on TV."

As soon as I've said it, I remember telling Mom I'd keep it a secret. That's something I ought to be able to manage. And now, I've shot off my big mouth.

"TV?" Alison says, sounding surprised. "As what?"

"Oh, nothing," I try to change the subject. "She's talking to a producer about being on some celebrity wedding show."

Gretchen's eyebrows shoot up. "Is your mom really that much of a celebrity?"

There's a note in her voice. One that I've heard a few times before. Caution, wariness. If we weren't friends, I might even say a little bit of jealousy.

"No," I say. "But she wants to be, I guess."

"What will you be doing?" Violet asks.

"I don't know. Making the wedding cake on TV maybe? You know, kids who cook are a thing now."

"Like *MasterChef Junior*?" Alison says. "Cool."

The others nod. Everyone, that is, except Gretchen. She's staring at the lemon and egg mixture in the bowl in front of her, stirring in the double cream like she's out to turn it black and blue.

As I watch Gretchen, I start to feel worried. Other than Violet, I consider her to be my best friend. Sure, we've had our issues, but overall I respect how cool and confident she is. For one thing, she's been the student council rep every semester for the last two years, and this year she's class president. She knows how to talk to grown-ups and always seems to be in control. She's as steady as a brick and the first person I'd go to in a crisis. Unless the crisis was between us.

"What's up?" I say, keeping my voice low. "What have I done wrong?"

"Nothing." She doesn't look up. "I'm glad things are going so well for you. TV—well, I don't think any of us expected that. I'm sure it will be fab when *you're* on there, making the wedding cake."

"I really don't know anything about it yet."

All of a sudden, I realize why she's angry. I said I will be making the cake, not "we." Even Violet looks a little bit hurt. "I thought we were all going to help make the cake," she says. "Don't you want our help?"

"I do!" I protest. "Definitely. But remember, this is Mom's thing, not mine. I never asked for it, and I don't want it—or this whole Bridezilla wedding."

Gretchen gives a little smirk. "You've hit the nail on the head, Scarlett. You want this, you don't want that. You wish things were this way and not that way. You're the blogger, you call the shots. We aren't a club anymore. We're Scarlett and her sidekicks." She lets go of her spoon and lets it sink into the mixture. We all watch openmouthed as she takes off her apron and throws it on to the table. "And you know what? I've had enough. It's been fun, but I'm out of here."

"Why are you doing this?" A chill creeps up my spine. "Just because of the ridiculous TV thing?"

Gretchen shakes her head. "No, that's not it." She looks at Alison. I do too. Alison puts down her spoon.

"The thing is, Scarlett, it's not the same as when we started," Alison says. "I mean, you've got the blog and the charity stuff. And the rest of us—well, I don't know."

"The rest of you?" I glance around from Violet to Nick. "You've been talking about this behind my back?"

"No, Scarlett," Nick says. "That's not fair."

"Fair? Is any of this fair?" I say in a raised voice. "I mean, all I did was turn up a little bit late tonight. I was so looking forward to baking something with you guys—I know I haven't had much time lately. And—foolish me—I thought I could tell you—my *friends*—about all the fuss with Mom and the wedding." I take off my apron and throw it down on top of Gretchen's. "I really could have used your support, but instead, you're all just ganging up on me."

"Look," Nick says, "everyone calm down. We're all here for the same reason."

I feel tears prickling behind my eyes. "Are we? I'm not sure anymore."

I turn back to Gretchen. "I think you should finish your lemon tarts. Because there's six of you and one of me. It doesn't take a genius to figure out who should stay and who should go."

I spin around and walk out of the kitchen, tears rolling down my face.

"Wait, Scarlett!" Violet runs after me and tries to grab my arm, but I wriggle away.

"No. Let me go. You take over the club. I quit."

"Come back—"

I slam the door behind me.

CHAPTER 8

Under the Apple Tree

I RUN TOWARD THE MAIN road. The sky is steel gray and the wind has picked up; tears stream down my face and my hair whips into my eyes. Breathing hard, I slow to a walk. I go past the shops—the diner, the dry cleaners, the hair salon—dodging people on their way home from work. Just past a pub, I turn down a tiny alleyway that twists and turns, and eventually comes to a little park that used to be the village green.

In one corner, there's a bench underneath a gnarled apple tree covered with white blossoms. I sit, staring at the sky through the branches. The wind blows a few blossoms down on to my head.

I know I'm probably acting silly—I should have stayed there and faced them. Tried to sort things out. But I feel like there's a giant weight pressing down on me—the wedding, the TV thing—and now I've messed things up with my friends too. Maybe they're right—maybe I am selling out. Maybe I am spending too much time on the blog and not enough time cooking, which is how everything got started in the first place. And then there's other stuff too. Like Nick, and the fact that I've no idea what's up with us—or if there is an us. And Violet...something's definitely bothering her, and I feel sad that she hasn't told me. And the really bad thing is...well, that I haven't asked.

I swallow hard, but the lump that's formed in my throat won't budge. A couple of pigeons begin to circle overhead, ducking and diving around the steeple of the old stone church across from the park. I watch them, listening to the sound of the wind in the tree and the traffic.

"Scarlett?" I jerk back to reality. Violet is walking toward me across the grass.

"Hi." A thousand emotions well up inside me, but I push them away. "How did you know I'd be here?"

"I didn't." She walks past me to the tree, touching the bark. "I come here sometimes when I want to be alone."

"Sorry," I say, taking the hint. "I'll go if you want me to."

"No, don't." She comes over to the bench and sits at the opposite end from me.

"Okay."

"And actually," she says, "today I came here because I was on my way to the shop to get some more edible glitter, and I spotted you."

In spite of everything, I can't help but laugh. "I get it," I say. "It would be tragic if you ran out of edible glitter."

Violet laughs too, and I start to feel a little better. But she stops before I do. I turn to face her. "Violet, is there something wrong? Do you want to talk about it?"

"No, it's nothing, really." She waves a hand. "Just some bad dreams I've been having lately. I'm not sleeping very well, so I'm really tired."

"Oh, what are—"

"Do you think that Fraser likes Alison?" she says, cutting me off.

"Fraser?" I look at her in surprise. Fraser was our first "boy" member other than Nick. He's a total computer geek. Which is probably why he figured out sooner than just about anyone else who was behind the *Secret Cooking Club*.

He first "came out" as a member of the club during the bake-off we had at our school for a charity for the elderly. He's been a regular ever since. He's a really nice guy—originally from Scotland. I've never heard him say a bad word about anyone, and, now that I think about it, I guess he is kind of cute.

"I don't know," I say. "I haven't really noticed."

"Whatever." She shrugs. Suddenly, everything makes sense—Violet's moods lately, and how she sometimes goes really quiet when we all meet up. I know because that's how I was—and sometimes still am—when I first met Nick.

"I don't know about Alison," I say, smiling broadly. "But now that I think about it, he'd be perfect for *you*. I mean, he's so nice—and cute too. I can totally see it."

"Really?" Her eyes spark with hope, but then her lips turn downward again. "I don't know." She sighs. "We've chatted a little bit—on Facebook and by text. Just regular stuff like what we're having for dinner and the cooking shows on TV." She pauses thoughtfully. "He's funny. And clever...but then..."

"But what?" I smile encouragingly. "It sounds great. I mean, Nick doesn't ask me what I'm having for dinner."

"But then, when we're with the group, he only seems to have eyes for one person. And it isn't me."

I want to reassure her that it's normal to feel jealous of other girls when you like a boy. Before I knew that Nick was Alison's cousin, I was convinced that he liked her—they were always laughing and chatting, and well...Alison's beautiful.

But somehow, I don't think telling Violet that is going to help very much.

"I haven't noticed him looking at Alison," I say. "I guess I haven't spent much time getting to know him. I've been so preoccupied with…well—everything. As Gretchen says, I've let all of you down."

"No," Violet says. "You haven't. I mean, you've got a lot going on. But I think you do have time for your friends. I respect that about you."

"Thanks." I realize uncomfortably that once again we're talking about me. "But what are you going to do about Fraser?"

"Do?" She looks horrified. "I'm not going to *do* anything. You can't tell anyone what I said. I think I'd die of mortification."

"I know the feeling. It's exactly how I felt about Nick when he first started helping me with the blog. I won't breathe a word."

"Thanks." She stands, looking relieved.

But my mind is already turning over ways that I can help my friend.

"Why don't you make him something special and surprise him?"

"Hmm," Violet considers. "That worked for you, didn't it? With Nick?"

I think of how I nervous and excited I felt when Nick first seemed to "notice" me. The Secret Cooking Club had been secretly leaving food and baked goods in the cafeteria at lunchtime, with a sign saying "free samples." One day, Nick saw me putting a basket in the cafeteria, when I was supposed to be on a bathroom break. That was the start of it, I guess. He helped me set up the blog, and we helped him make a beautiful rainbow cake for his mom's birthday.

I still feel nervous-excited around Nick and still don't know if I'm his girlfriend or not. But I do know that without the Secret Cooking Club, we might never even have spoken to each other.

"I wouldn't exactly say it's worked," I say. "But it's been a step in the right direction."

"Well, I think it has." Violet smiles mischievously. "Maybe you need to be a little braver too and ask him what's up."

"Ask him?" I stare at her in horror. It strikes me how I'm pretty good at giving advice, and not very good at taking it. I've tried to convince myself that I'm happy the way things are going with Nick and that I don't need some kind of label on the relationship.

"Yeah." Violet grins. "It's not so easy, is it?"

She walks off to the shop to buy the edible glitter. The

wind blows more apple blossoms down on my head, like a showering of confetti. But right now, unfortunately, there's not much to celebrate.

CHAPTER 9

An Unknown Sender

I FEEL BETTER AFTER TALKING with Violet and finding out what's bothering her. But the next day at school, I'm still upset about what happened with Gretchen and the others. Instead of focusing on the discussion of Shakespeare's sonnets and the death of William the Conqueror, I replay the last few months in my head. Between the blog, the cooking videos we've made for the site, and helping tweet and publicize other charity bake-offs, the Secret Cooking Club hasn't had a lot of time to do the thing we do best. But is that really my fault?

After school, both Violet and Naya try to convince me to go to the senior center with the others to drop off the treats we've made. I tell them I'm not feeling very well—not far from the truth—and go home. With each step I take, I feel more and more guilty. I've made friends with a few of the elderly residents at the home—we all have. I should have swallowed my pride and gone with the others for their sake, if nothing else. And also, I posted the blog post about baking for the senior center—which made it sound like everything's wonderful. By staying away, I'm only proving Gretchen right.

And then another thought pops into my head. I wonder if Mom started out her original blog with good intentions, only to have it morph into something unrecognizable? I know she was trying to be a good mom—reaching out to other parents—and also earn a living to support her family. She went wrong along the way by writing "funny/embarrassing" things about me, and refusing to see how much I hated it. It was awful—and hurtful. But now that I'm on the other side, I'm starting to think that maybe I've made the opposite mistake. Instead of being too truthful, I'm trying too hard to make things sound better than they are. I've set myself apart and made my friends believe that I think it's all about me.

I stop walking and take out my phone. I'll text Violet—and Gretchen—and all the other members. Say sorry. Ask for another chance. We can meet up and talk things through. Surely Gretchen would go along with something so grown-up sounding.

As I'm about to type the message, I notice a little envelope on the screen—a new message from an unknown sender. I open it and read:

Hi, honey, how are things? I ran into your mom today and she gave me your number. I'm back living in town and thought maybe I could take you and your sister out for a pizza. There's a great little place just around the corner from me. Maybe we can go on Saturday? Can't wait to see you soon.

Love, Dad

Dad.

I stare down at the signature. If I hadn't fallen out with my friends, I might have thought that one of them was playing a joke on me. For the last several years, Dad has been living in the city with his girlfriend. I had no idea that he was back here. Or that Mom "ran into" him and gave him my number.

I go inside the house and thunk down my bag in the hall. "Scarlett?" Mom calls. "Is that you?"

"Yeah," I say. In the kitchen, Mom is unloading a couple of plastic supermarket bags (she never remembers to bring bags with her and always grumbles about having to pay the plastic bag fee). "You okay?" I help unload the bags. There are a few frozen pizzas, some yogurts, a bunch of bananas, cat food for Treacle, and—unbelievably—three more bride magazines.

"I'm great," Mom says. "You want pizza tonight?"

"Um…" When she first found out about the Secret Cooking Club, Mom turned over a new leaf, cooking at least a few meals a week that didn't involve frozen or microwave food. I helped, of course, and Mom wrote a few "inspirational" blog posts about the value of cooking together. We even made a vlog of her and me cooking a chicken dish and we each posted it on our website. That was what…January, maybe? February?

When did we stop?

"I was thinking of making a curry," I say. "We've got a new member of the club at school—Naya. She gave me a great recipe that I'd like to try."

"A curry?" Mom puts the frozen food in the already overflowing freezer and switches the kettle on. "Is curry healthy? Because I really need to drop a dress size or two before the wedding."

I don't bother to point out that curry is probably healthier than frozen pizza—most things are. Instead, I smile reassuringly. "I wouldn't worry, Mom. I think you look fine."

She shakes her head and tsks. For a moment, I imagine that I can see the green scales of the "Momster" coming to the surface underneath the skin of her face. "I may look fine to you, Scarlett," she says, "but I'm going to be on TV. The camera adds ten pounds."

"Does it?" I puzzle over this.

"Yes. And since you haven't asked, I'll tell you about my meeting with the producer—unless you're running off next door or something."

"No, I'm not." *Unfortunately.*

"It's all going ahead—it's going to be fantastic. I'll be featured on *Wedding Belles*—I'll have a camera following me around while I'm getting ready for the wedding. They'll also do a feature on my blog. And they definitely want you girls too."

"Oh."

"So I've made an appointment at my salon. We'll get you both haircuts and manicures." She peers at my face. "And maybe have your eyebrows plucked. Then, we'll go for our first fitting."

"Fitting?"

"For my wedding dress and your bridesmaid's dress." She makes it sound like I'm completely dense. "I've made five appointments for Saturday. It will be such fun."

Such fun.

"Yeah, sounds great," I lie. "There is one thing, though."

Mom's eyes look reptilian as she gives me "the stare." I guess she's worried that I might upset her carefully made plans. "What?"

"It's just—well…Dad texted me," I say. "He said he ran into you. He wants to take Kelsie and me for pizza on Saturday."

"Yes—that's fine." Mom waves her bejeweled hand. "We'll all meet up after the fittings—that's what I told him."

"You did?" I lean back in surprise. "Why?"

"Because he's your dad, of course. I ran into him at the TV station. He's heading up some new IT upgrade there. It was a surprise, but I knew he was back in town."

"Oh. Um, do I have to see him?"

She slams a coffee cup down on the counter. "Yes, Scarlett. Haven't I told you that we can't just run away from our problems? Dad's affected by this too. He's split up with his…" She pauses, like she's going to say something rude, finally settling on "girlfriend." "And naturally, since he's back, in town," she adds, "he wants to see more of you and Kelsie."

"Naturally," I grumble.

"Anyway, I thought it would be fun to get together." She gives a little laugh. "Old times' sake and all that. Besides, it's his birthday on Saturday. I thought maybe you and your cooking club could make him a cake."

"You want *me* to make *him* a cake?" This is just wrong on so many levels.

"Yes, why not?" She looks genuinely surprised at my reaction. "It will be really nice. He's your *dad*."

Shaking my head, I decide it's best just to give in. "Fine," I say. "Whatever."

CHAPTER 10

The. Cake.

EVERYTHING WAS GOING SO WELL—just days ago, it seems. But now, things have turned on their head. How did that happen, and why?

Violet and Alison post photos of the visit to the old people's home to our Instagram page. It's lovely to see so many happy, smiling faces among the elderly residents. But there's a sadness tugging inside of me that refuses to go away. I should have been there with them. And maybe I would have been, if Dad's message hadn't come from out of the blue and thrown me totally off balance.

He's your dad…

I mean, obviously, I know that. But just because he's back in town and wants to "see more" of me and my sister, doesn't mean that's what I want. Mom's about to marry Em-K and that's a big thing. Then there's the wedding and the TV show—Dad's "return" couldn't have come at a worse time.

After school, I walk home by myself via the corner shop. I need to get some flour and icing sugar for *the cake*—which right now seems like the focus of all my problems. The bell tinkles as I enter and make my way to the tiny baking aisle. I find the flour and the icing sugar, but instead of grabbing them and going to the cashier, I hesitate. On the shelf next to the dry ingredients is a row of cake mixes in boxes, and next to those, packets of icing.

I pick up one of the boxes: devil's food chocolate cake. It looks okay—there's a picture of a smiling woman on the box and a creamy-looking cake with squiggles of steam coming off it. I check the instructions. All that's required is to stir the mix in with a couple of eggs, some water, and some oil. Easy-peasy—

"Scarlett?"

I freeze for a nanosecond, then spring into action—shoving the box of cake mix back on the shelf. It knocks into the one behind, and the boxes collapse like dominoes, several falling on to the floor. I grab the icing sugar and the flour.

"Hi, Nick," I say, my face on fire. "Just had to pick up a few things for a cake I'm making."

"Sorry—didn't mean to startle you."

"Oh, um, you didn't." I bend down and pick up the boxes of cake mix—the smiling woman's face now seems like she's accusing me of something. I put them back on the nearest shelf and, forcing a smile, make my way to the checkout.

The icing sugar and flour won't fit in my bag—I practically break the zip trying to get it closed. Nick wanders out of the shop, pretending not to notice how flustered I am. I pay at the register and go outside.

He's waiting for me there on the pavement, reading something on his phone. A strand of dark hair has fallen over his eyes. He pushes it back and looks at me with concern.

"You know—it would have been fine if you'd bought the cake mix."

"I know." I hang my head, feeling foolish. The conversation I had with Violet looms in my mind. I should talk to Nick about us—but right now, I feel too caught out. "It's just…" I stammer, "I've lost all my friends—other than Violet—and I don't want to mess up the blog too. I don't think using a cake mix would quite fit with it."

"Hey, come on." He reaches out, taking my hand. "You haven't lost *all* your friends."

"Oh really?" I snatch my hand away. "Gretchen might disagree."

"Come on, Scarlett, you know how she is," he challenges. "The second she's not the center of attention, it's like the world is out to get her."

I stare at him—I've never heard him say a mean word against anyone—and few people would *dare* to say a bad thing about Gretchen. "You really think that?"

"Maybe." He shrugs. "Who's the cake for?"

I sense he's trying to change the subject, and decide to let him. Right now, I need someone to talk to. "It's for my dad," I say. "It's his birthday on Saturday."

Nick's brows narrow. "You mean Em-K? I thought we made him a cake a month or so back."

The memory makes me smile. We made Em-K a deliciously moist carrot cake (with no nuts or raisins), and Violet and Alison made a little vegetable garden out of fondant with carrots, lettuce, tomatoes, and a hose and wheelbarrow. It was really cool—and it got lots of retweets—even by a few celeb chefs. But that was then. This is now…

"Not Em-K." I sigh. "My dad."

I tell him the whole story—what I know of it, at least. About how he and Mom used to fight a lot, but then he left us, and moved to the big city. About how Mom was really hurt by him going, and I guess I was too. And I tried really hard to put him out of my mind. About how he's now back in town and "ran into Mom" at the TV station. And now we're supposed to go with him for pizza after a day of wedding dress fittings— and, like, how weird is that?

Nick's frown deepens. "Maybe she wants to smooth things over with him," he says. "Make sure he's fine with the idea of her marrying someone else."

"Maybe," I say. "But would it matter if he wasn't fine with it? I mean, it shouldn't. As far as I'm concerned, Dad's out of our lives—and good riddance."

"Is that really what you think?"

"Yeah," I answer without any hesitation.

We walk along in silence. I know that Nick is only trying to make things better. I appreciate that about him. That…and a lot of other things. Though I wish that he'd be a little bit less worried about my feelings, and more worried about me being his girlfriend. But for now, I'm just really glad that he's here.

"Do you want me to help you make the cake?" he says.

"Yeah!" I brighten instantly. "If you've got time."

"Sure. It will be fun."

We walk to my house, chatting about school and about

what kind of decorations to put on the cake. Kelsie once said she thought it was weird that a boy wanted to join a cooking club. But when I pointed out how some of the best bakers on *The Great British Bake Off* are men, she seemed to get it. For Kelsie, that show is like heaven—I mean, it's TV and cake—two of her three favorite things. The other being ketchup, which she eats on practically everything.

"What's your dad into?" Nick asks as I open the door.

"I don't know," I say truthfully. "Before the stuff happened, he worked and went to the gym a lot. Though, I did have a kind of weird memory," I say. "Like, once he made us a big dinner of spaghetti Bolognese. It was really good."

I'm expecting him to laugh—after all, it's not hard to make good spaghetti Bolognese. But he looks thoughtful.

"So you think he might be interested in cooking?"

"I don't have a clue!"

"Hey…no worries." This time Nick does laugh. "I'm not saying you guys might have *something in common*."

"Ha-ha." I punch him lightly in the arm. "Very funny."

He turns to look at me, and once again I feel that electric *something* between us. I look away so that he can't see me blushing.

When we come into the house, my sister is in the front

room watching TV, with Treacle purring on her lap. "Hey, Kels." I stick my head in the room, straining to make myself heard over the sound of *Scooby-Doo*. "Do you want to help bake a cake?"

"A cake?" She doesn't take her eyes off the screen. "Um…"

"Come on, Kelsie," Nick says.

"Nick!" My sister squeals. She jumps up and rushes over to give him a hug. He picks her up and whirls her around.

"Let's go," Nick says, setting her down. "Turn that off, okay?"

"'Course!" Kelsie immediately switches the TV off. I give a little smirk. Whatever my relationship with Nick is or isn't, no one has a bigger crush on him than my little sister.

"Is Mom home?" I ask her as we're walking to the kitchen.

"Nope," she says. "But look what they did." She points, but it's not really necessary. Just inside the door to the kitchen, there's a gaping hole in the wall. The plaster is jagged and rough, the bricks at the edge smashed through. There's a trail of dust and a dirty wheelbarrow track leading across our kitchen floor and out of the back door.

"Oh right." I look at Nick. There's dust all over the kitchen—it doesn't look like it's really fit for baking anything. And on the other side of the opening, Rosemary's kitchen beckons like a magical world through the mist.

"Well, that makes things easier," Nick says. "Shall we clean up here, or go to Rosemary's kitchen?"

I smile. "Let's go through the wall."

I feel like I'm climbing through the wardrobe to Narnia or something as I follow Kelsie and Nick through the jagged opening.

"Are we going to have two kitchens?" Kelsie asks. I take the icing sugar and flour out of my bag.

"No, I think they'll make our old kitchen into a dining room or something," I say.

"So this will be our kitchen."

"Yeah."

"Fab," my sister says.

Nick and I get the ingredients out, and he helps my sister do the measuring. He naturally assumes that we're using the cake recipe from our special recipe book. It isn't very complex or different from other cake recipes—it has the same flour, butter, eggs, and sugar as in any other cookbook. But there's something about the handwritten recipes in the little red-and-green marbled notebook that seem to make everything taste better.

I know the cake will taste amazing—moist, fluffy, never dry or soggy. But right now, in a way, I wish we weren't using our special recipe. I don't want Dad to get any funny ideas. I start getting things ready to make the icing and the decorations—we'll stick to buttercream icing and sprinkles, nothing too fancy.

Kelsie pours the ingredients into the bowl and mixes them with her skinny arm. Nick even lets her break the eggs, which is something I never do. She quickly gets tired of stirring and asks Nick with her big, blue, puppy-dog eyes if he'll take over.

"Sure." He flexes his arm muscles and gives her a wink.

Kelsie sits and watches him. "Is Scarlett your girlfriend?" she asks out of the blue.

"Kelsie!" I blurt out. My skin crawls with mortification. "You don't ask people things like that."

She turns to look at me. "Why not? I mean, he's your boyfriend, right?"

Nick laughs awkwardly. I can feel the flush creeping down my neck.

"Yeah," he says, eyes fixed on the spoon swirling in the bowl. "She is."

"Oh, I thought so," Kelsie says. I feel a tremor flowing through my body. Does he mean it, or is he just putting my sister off? I wish she'd go back and watch TV. On second thought…she'd better not leave. "Scarlett's always talking about you. She goes this funny red color."

"Does she?" He winks at my sister. "I never noticed that before."

I force myself to laugh it off too, but I can't look at him. I can almost *feel* the spark between us, even though I'm standing a good three feet away from him.

"All mixed, I think," Nick says. "Scarlett, do you have the pan?"

I have to turn around and face him. Kelsie's staring at me. "Yeah—here." I hand him the pan that I've greased with butter. I look away quickly, but it's too late. My cheeks and face are bright red, and this time, I know he's noticed!

CHAPTER 11

Secrets and Lies

THE ROOM FEELS VERY WARM as I put the cake pan in the oven and turn the knob to set the timer.

"I'm going to go watch TV," Kelsie says. "'Kay?"

"You go, girl," Nick says.

I wipe my hands on my apron as Kelsie goes back though the hole in the wall to "our house." Maybe I should feel grateful to my sister for breaking the ice, but right now I'm both thankful and furious with her, in equal measure. Above all, I wish she'd stayed. Left alone with Nick, I'm tongue-tied. I go over to the counter and get the butter, icing sugar, vanilla, and milk ready to put in a bowl for the buttercream icing.

"You didn't have to say that." I can't look at him.

"She's eight," Nick says. "I had to say something. And besides, I mean, I know we haven't talked about it, and stuff, but…" I steal a look at him. He's blushing too.

I don't know what I was hoping for, but I'm pretty sure this isn't it. "Hey, don't worry about it," I say.

"No, that's not it." He takes a step toward me. I hold my breath. "It's just, I like things the way they are. I don't want to mess them up…" He lifts his shoulders and lets out a breath. "This is…um…awkward."

I bridge the distance between us. "I don't want things to be awkward either." I put my hand on his arm. "So let's just forget it, okay?"

He shakes his head. "I think the cat's out of the bag, don't you?"

He takes my arms and gently pulls me to him, so close that his dark hair tickles my face. I can feel electricity racing up and down my spine, and I'm sure that he must be able to hear the drumming of my heart. *OMG, he's going to kiss me!* My knees go wobbly, and at the same time, my body goes rigid. *Does my breath smell bad? Why didn't I brush my teeth when I got—*

"Hello? Anybody home?"

I take a giant step back from Nick, smoothing my hands

on my apron, trying to breathe and ignore my heart doing jumping jacks in my chest. Nick steps away too, and I can see he's as embarrassed as I am.

"Anybody—"

"We're in here," I say.

Em-K sticks his head through the hole in the wall. "Whew," he says. "Didn't your mom ask the workmen to clean up?" He climbs through. "I thought they were putting in a door."

"I don't know," I say in answer to both questions.

He frowns and checks the screen of his phone. "She texted me that she would be here—let's see—an hour ago. I would have thought she'd be here by now."

His fingers tap quickly over the screen.

I go over to the table and check my phone. "I got a text from her about fifteen minutes ago," I say. "Sorry—I didn't hear it come in. She says she popped out to meet a friend and will be back around eight."

"Oh." Em-K's face falls. "I left early to get here. I guess I'll go and do some work while I'm waiting." He sniffs the air. "What's that you're making?" he says. "Smells wonderful."

"It's a cake," Nick says.

"It's…um…Nick's dad's birthday tomorrow," I add quickly. My eyes flick to him and back to Em-K.

"Is it?" He frowns. "I thought you did a cake for him a few months back." He shakes his head. "I must be going senile."

"That was for my brother," Nick jumps in to the rescue. "It was his birthday."

"Ah." Em-K heads back to the hole in the wall. "Maybe that was it." His dark head disappears back into our section of the house.

As soon as he's gone, my knees feel weak with relief. "Thanks," I whisper to Nick.

Nick shakes his head as the oven starts beeping. "Are you sure lying to him is a good idea?"

"What am I supposed to do? Mom's run off, and I'm here baking a cake for my dad. Do you think I'm happy about it?"

Nick opens the oven door. The steam feels clean and pure against my face. He slides out the rack, and I poke the cake with a sharp knife to see if it's done in the middle. The knife comes out clean. "Done," I say.

He takes out the cake and sets the pan on a wire rack to cool.

We stand there staring at each other across the cake. He knows I feel bad and I know he feels bad for me. It's a long way from where we were only a few minutes ago.

"I should go," he says, looking at his watch. "I told Mom I'd be home for dinner."

"Okay." I'm a little upset and a lot relieved that he's going. "I'll put the icing and sprinkles on when it cools."

We walk together back to the hole in the wall, but he pulls me up short. "Let me know how it goes tomorrow with… the cake."

"I will. And thanks…" I pause, feeling like I'm drowning in his eyes, "…for everything."

"My pleasure." He gives me a quick kiss on the cheek, and skillfully avoids any further awkwardness by disappearing back through the hole in the wall.

I stand there for a long time staring at the hole, listening to the sound of Em-K shuffling papers and typing on his laptop—it's like he's a million miles away. Eventually I turn back to the cake cooling on the rack. I release the springs on the cake pan and let the cake cool some more.

By the time the cake is cool and I'm spreading buttercream icing over it, I hear sounds from my own kitchen. Mom's voice—and Em-K's. I try not to listen. It's like they're talking through water. Mom is pleasant, telling him how she "ran into an old friend" and went for coffee.

Em-K sounds unusually cold and stressed. "You know I'm

going to be away for at least a week, Claire. I thought we were supposed to have dinner tonight."

I think about the lie I told, and whether it will come back to bite me. And I think about Nick—even after every stomach-flipping moment tonight, I'm still not sure if we're boyfriend and girlfriend. I don't understand how Violet wants this kind of stress with a boy.

"And this TV thing," Em-K continues. "I know you really want to do it. But do you think it's best—for us and the girls? Does Scarlett want to do it?"

"Of course," Mom snaps. "Why wouldn't she?"

As I go upstairs, not bothering to listen anymore, I think about how I wish this wedding would hurry up and come soon, so it will be over. Then I can get back to focusing on fixing things with my friends, making delicious food with the Secret Cooking Club, and basically just getting on with normal life.

Whatever that is.

CHAPTER 12

Bonbons and Boutiques

ON SATURDAY MORNING, MOM WAKES me out of a deep sleep. "Come on, Scarlett," she says. "We've got a big day ahead."

"Yeah, Mom," I grumble, wishing I could bury myself under the duvet for a few more minutes—or even hours—or better yet, skip today altogether. But I know that tone in Mom's voice—half excitement, half stress: total focus. Today's the day she's going to find the perfect wedding dress, and nothing—certainly not me—is going to stop her.

Mom goes downstairs to make coffee, and Kelsie comes into my room. "Come on, slowpoke," my sister says. "Get up."

I throw my old teddy bear at her and swing out of bed.

"It's going to be so cool!" she says. "I can't wait to start trying on dresses! It's so *exciting*."

"That's one word for it."

She runs downstairs, and I give in and get dressed. I know that Mom and Kelsie are dying to go wedding shopping. Which is great—for them. But try as I might, I can't get excited about trying on some itchy, hot dress in a hideous color that I'll never wear again. *I'm doing this for Mom*, I remind myself.

To hurry things along, Mom's made breakfast: a squeezie packet of blueberry and oat purée each, and a rack of burnt toast to share.

"Um, do you want me to make some eggs?" I offer.

"No time," Mom says, gulping down a cup of coffee. "We're all due at my hair salon for a cut and style. Then we're visiting four bridal shops. The first three on our own—just to get the flavor of it—and then the camera crew is meeting us at the last one."

My stomach twists. "They're filming us at the fittings?"

"Obviously. That's what the show is about—preparing for the perfect fairy-tale wedding. Every bride wants to feel like a princess. The viewers will want to see me finding the perfect dress."

"Right. I…guess I didn't think of it like that."

"And of course, they'll want to film you too. I mean, you and Kelsie are my bridesmaids. We'll find lovely dresses for you both." She drinks her cup of black coffee in one gulp.

"And Em-K? Is he getting filmed too?"

"Well, no. It's about brides—you know, a girly thing."

"But he's okay with it?"

She gives me a sharp glance. "Of course. Why wouldn't he be?"

"Uh…no reason."

"We agreed last night that the wedding will be in eight weeks," she says as she searches her bag for her car keys. "That fits in with the filming schedule."

"Sure, Mom." I don't bother to point out that it's a tad unromantic that Mom's perfect fairy-tale wedding has to be rushed to fit in with a TV schedule. In fact, I decide it's safest not to point out anything at all.

Getting our hair done seems to take forever. Mom chats away to the stylist about the wedding, the blog, her product lines in stores, and her husband-to-be. Kelsie fidgets and cries out when the stylist tries to untangle her unruly blond hair, and I sit there bored out of my skull. By the time we've finished, my hair does look better—the split ends have been cut off and it actually has a shape—and more than anything, I wish we could just go home and have a normal Saturday. But of course, that's not to be. As we leave the hair salon, I have a sinking feeling in my stomach about the rest of the day—the fittings, the filming, and then, like the icing on *the cake*…dinner with Dad.

It takes us almost forty-five minutes to drive to the first bridal "boutique." The shop looks tiny—in one window at the side of the door there's a tacky Cinderella wedding dress with lace and sparkles. "Wow!" Kelsie puts her hand to her mouth. "It's so beautiful. You have to get that one, Mom."

Mom laughs and ruffles Kelsie's hair. "That one is nice, Kels." She then points to the dress in the other window—a long, elegant silk dress with a neckline of tiny pearls. "But that's more what I had in mind."

"It's pretty, Mom." My spirits lift. Maybe Mom will choose something tasteful after all.

"Yes, well…" She shakes her head like she's now decided to reject it. "It probably won't suit me."

When we enter the shop, a woman in a black pantsuit comes out from the back. "Welcome to Sophie's Brides," she says, sweeping a hand that sparkles with rings. "I'm Sophie. We're so honored that you've chosen us to help make your 'happily ever after' come true." Her glance snags on my sister, who has discovered a crystal dish of bonbons by the counter. The woman frowns briefly as my sister shoves a handful in her mouth.

"Thanks," Mom says. "You have a lovely shop." She goes over to the rack and starts flipping through the dresses, touching the delicate fabrics. Sophie's frown deepens, like Mom's doing something wrong. Her perfume wafts as she quickly goes over to Mom. "If you tell me what you have in mind for your dress, perhaps I can select a perfect assortment of dresses for you to try on."

"Sure." Mom hangs on to the puffy net skirt she's holding, running her finger over the tiny gems sewn in. "Maybe I could try this one. Or the Cinderella one in the window."

So much for good taste.

"Hmm," the woman says. "I'm not sure that style would suit you."

"Oh." Mom's face reddens. "Of course, you know best."

"How about this one?" The woman holds out an ivory silk dress similar to the one I liked.

"That is nice," Mom says. "What's the price on that one?"

Sophie purses her lips and holds up the tag between two fingers like it's a dirty tissue.

Mom can't quite hide a gasp.

"You must remember," Sophie says, "that your special day is a once-in-a-lifetime experience."

"Well, twice, in my case." Mom laughs awkwardly. "But the first time was a bit of a mess, so maybe it doesn't count."

"Of course." The woman sniffs. This whole thing is clearly not a marriage "made in heaven," so I wish we could just leave.

Mom flips through a few more dresses, raising her eyebrows at another price tag.

"And remember," the woman adds, "we cater to a very exclusive clientele. Everything is bespoke. That means it's custom-made just for you. For most of my customers, the prices are very reasonable."

Mom turns to her. "Of course," she says. "I understand completely. And as my fiancé is a congressman, money isn't an object. I'm really just asking for my followers. I'm doing a post this week on wedding shopping. You've might have heard of my blog: *Mindfulness for Moms*?"

"I'm afraid not."

I sense that Mom's about to embarrass herself, trying to somehow impress snooty old Sophie. Before that can happen, I interrupt: "Uh, Mom," I say, "sorry, but I think we need to get on to our next appointment…"

I brace myself, worried that Bridezilla might make a guest appearance. But surprisingly, Mom actually looks grateful.

"Thanks for the reminder," she says. She gives Sophie a pained smile.

"But, Mom," Kelsie says. "You haven't tried on the Cinderella dress." She pops the last bonbon into her mouth, leaving the dish empty.

"Sorry, darling," Mom says. "But I'm thinking actually I might want something more along the lines of Snow White. Right, Scarlett?" She gives me a pointed smile.

"Right." I keep my eyes glued to the plush carpet, and follow Mom and Kelsie out of the shop.

After the first painful experience, I'm hoping Mom will decide to skip the other shops. But if anything, she seems even keener, and things go from bad to worse. We visit two more bridal shops, each fancier than the first. Mom fingers the dresses, tsks over the prices, tries to impress the sales assistants with her *congressman* fiancé, and somehow, despite her enthusiasm, doesn't try on a single dress. By the time we finally grab lunch (the McDonald's in the parking lot of the shopping center), Kelsie is beside herself with all the lovely dresses that Mom has fawned over ("you're right, Kels, I would feel like a princess"), fobbed off ("maybe I'm not Snow White—maybe more of a

Princess Anna?"), and ultimately rejected ("let's look at the next place, then I'll decide"). I'm just fed up because if she doesn't find *the dress* today, then we'll have to do this all over again.

"Maybe you can try on one of the dresses, Mom," I say, trying to sound cheerful. "I'm sure you'd look lovely, and you'll get an idea of what suits you. And just think, you can post it on your blog or Instagram page!" If that doesn't convince her, then nothing will.

"You're right, Scarlett." She wipes the grease from her Big Mac off her chin. "I do owe that to my followers. It's just—I don't know." Her smile edges down into a frown. "Nothing seems quite right somehow."

"What doesn't?" Suddenly, I feel hopeful again. Maybe Mom's finally coming to her senses. Realizing that her first idea—eloping to a beach to get married in flip-flops and her white summer dress with the blue flowers that she bought on sale—is the best solution all around.

"Those shops," she says huffily. "I mean, really, does every saleswoman at a bridal shop have a stick up her bottom or something?"

I giggle—as much at Kelsie's shocked face as at the comment. "I agree," I say. "They were awful."

Mom waves her hand. "I can see now why all the best

people have their dresses custom-made specially. You know—like Kate Middleton. That's what I should do."

"Um, yeah." I swallow hard. Surely Mom can't be comparing her wedding to Kate Middleton's! "But even the 'best people' probably have to try on a few styles to find the right one."

"Yes, yes." She nudges Kelsie to hurry up eating her fries (she's already gone through six packets of ketchup). "I'm sure you're right. In any case, we'd better get going. The film crew is meeting us at the next shop."

The film crew. I groan inwardly. I don't dare break it to her that Kate Middleton probably didn't have photographers filming her in her underwear during her wedding dress fittings. But then again, Mom's always been a martyr where her followers are concerned.

CHAPTER 13

Lights, Camera, Action!

AS SOON AS WE PULL into the packed parking lot, it's obvious that the Bridal Center is not like the posh bridal shops. It's a cross between Forever 21 and a circus. The place is completely chaotic with Saturday-afternoon shoppers, and the enormous lights and cameras are in the way of everyone. There's a table piled high with cut fruit, cookies, sandwiches, and bottled water, and the camera crew—two scruffy-looking guys with long hair wearing band T-shirts—are testing out the sound and the lighting. We're barely inside the door when a short, ginger-haired woman—who is, I realize, the producer Mom's been talking to—rushes up to Mom and hugs her.

"Oh, Claire—right on time. We're *so* looking forward to this!"

"Thanks, Poppy," Mom says, smiling. "Me too."

Still standing close to Mom, the producer sniffs the air. "What's that I smell—did your daughter cook you one of those fantastic gourmet meals I've heard so much about?"

"We had McDonald's," Kelsie says.

"Well, uh, we were in a hurry to get here," Mom covers. She flashes my sister a glare. "Besides, Scarlett's been busy baking and trying out all sorts of recipes for the wedding cake. Right, darling?"

"Ouch!" I cry out at the poke in the ribs. "Uh, right."

"Great…" The producer looks at me, the enthusiasm ebbing from her face. "Well, anyway, we've got some great dresses picked out for you to try on, Claire. It's going to be such fun! Now, let's get you to makeup."

"Right!" The producer links arms with Mom and takes her off to a little table set up with a huge makeup kit. Any worries about what the "best people" do and any questions about whether Kate Middleton would have done some price comparison shopping at the Bridal Center seem to have gone right out the window.

"Let's have a look around," I say to Kelsie. "Looks like we'll be here for a while."

I follow my sister over to the food table, where she

pockets a handful of cookies and shoves some strawberries into her mouth. I take some grapes and a bottle of water. The other customers in the shop walk past us warily. Maybe they're wondering if they ought to recognize Mom—or her kids. Wondering if we're the "best people"—in spite of the fact that we look normal.

Kelsie makes a beeline over to the jewelry section and starts trying on tiaras. "I love weddings," she says. "I want to get married so many times—just like Mom."

"Um, I don't think that's the point," I say. A shop assistant gives us a look. I try to take the crown off Kelsie's head, but the combs get tangled in her hair. With a shriek, she pulls away and runs over to the shoe section. She takes off her sandal and shoves her foot into one of the white satin display models. "Look, it's my glass slipper!" she says, parading around.

"Kelsie!" I hiss, but just then, one of the cameramen comes over.

"Hey, Jed, let's get a shot of this. Can you put that tiara back on?" he says to my sister.

OMG. As if one second-time bride and TV-star wannabe wasn't enough for one family, now I've got two!

Ignoring the protests of the shop manager, my sister puts on another of the display shoes (both left feet), grabs a few ropes of pearls and puts them around her neck, and starts dancing around and singing "Let It Go" at the top of her lungs.

There's only two good things about the afternoon. One is that Mom actually has to try on some dresses. She quickly rejects the puffy, lacy, over-the-top dresses (upon the recommendation of the TV stylist) and tries on a few more sensible straight and A-line dresses. She's short and thin, and even the white satin heels can't do much to change that. But when she tries on the wedding dresses, with Kelsie fawning over her and me standing silently in the background nodding or shaking my head, she does seem younger—and happy. It's nice to see. And the camera doesn't seem to make her nervous at all. But after she's tried on about fifteen dresses, the "hitch" comes.

"Can we get some footage of your daughters trying on bridesmaids' dresses?" Poppy, the producer, asks.

"Oh. can we, Mom?" my sister yells.

Mom does a second twirl in front of the mirror in a tight-fitting silk dress with a "mermaid" tail. She checks her watch. "Maybe one or two," she says. "Then we've got a dinner engagement."

The knot inside me tightens. The second "good" thing

about the afternoon, is that it's not this evening—when we're supposed to meet up with Dad.

"What are your colors?" the producer asks. She and Mom chat about lilac versus lavender and pink versus peach. I slip out and over to the rack of bridesmaids' dresses to try to do damage control—pick out something that won't be too hideous. I flip through the racks as two of the stylists come over to me. "It's okay, dear," one of them says. "Come over to makeup and we'll get you sorted."

By the time it's over, I feel like my face is about to crack from faking a smile and trying to act like the whole thing is not completely horrendous. It's worse than the days of the blog—much worse, in fact. The camera makes my skin crawl, and thinking about people watching me parading in around in the awful dresses Mom chooses—lilac, peach, lavender, pink—makes me feel like throwing up. Luckily, my sister was "a natural" in front of the camera, and my only hope is that they'll focus on her. If not, well…I can't be held responsible for my actions.

I'd just finished changing back into my jeans and T-shirt when Producer Poppy cornered me on the way out of the dressing room.

"Now, Scarlett, before you go, we must speak about the wedding cake film shoot."

"Um, yeah," I say, wishing the salmon-pink carpet of the changing room area would open up and swallow me whole. "Sounds good."

"There's a lot to do in a very short time—we need to have our best game faces on," she says. "So how about I have my assistant give you a call in the next day or two to arrange things? Her name is Annie."

"Um, yeah," I repeat. "Sounds good."

She gives me a worried glance, but just then there's a loud clatter and thunk. I turn toward the fitting rooms and see that another bride-to-be has exited to parade around in front of the mirror, and her huge skirt has swished into one of the lamps that the cameramen are using and knocked it over. The light is so hot that the lace and ruffles start to singe and smoke, until Producer Poppy rushes over and throws a jug of lemon water on it.

I take advantage of the distraction to go back out to the main part of the shop to wait for Mom.

By the time we finally leave the Bridal Center, I'm exhausted, and I can actually feel my skin breaking out under all that makeup. But right now, I can't even think about that. Not when dinner with Dad is looming in my mind.

CHAPTER 14

Happy Families

MOM IS FRAZZLED AND IRRITABLE as we leave the Bridal Center. "I'm so glad that's over," she says.

"Really?" I say, surprised. "But you liked the dresses, right? I mean, you looked good."

"Oh, I don't know. I'm just tired. And you, young lady"—she glances at my sister in the rearview mirror—"need to learn to behave."

Kelsie barely looks up from the game she's playing on Mom's phone. I wish I was as easily distracted as my sister. We pull into the parking lot of the restaurant. Bernini's—I realize with a sinking heart that it's the same restaurant where Em-K proposed to Mom. At the time, I'd thought it was "romantic" that Mom had never come here with anyone else. Obviously, she must not see it that way.

I get out of the car and go around to the trunk to get the cake. Before getting out, Mom checks her makeup and hair in the car mirror. To me it seems a little weird that she'd care what Dad thinks. Though Alison would probably say that it's normal to want to impress your ex. She'd know—she's had a few boyfriends before.

The plastic cake container feels heavy as a brick as I lift it out. In the end, I covered the whole cake with buttercream icing and blue, yellow, and pink sprinkles. I didn't put any writing on it, or even "happy birthday." It's the most joyless cake I've ever made.

Kelsie runs on ahead into the restaurant to look for Dad.

"Come on, Scarlett." Mom's tone makes it sound like I'm dragging my feet. "Let's go inside."

The restaurant is dark and noisy. The tables have red-and-white checkered cloths on them with drippy wax candles set in wine bottles wrapped in straw. As I enter, Kelsie makes a beeline for a round table near the back of the restaurant, practically knocking down a waitress carrying a tray.

"Daddy!" she yells.

"Hi, Kels Bels!" a familiar voice replies. Dad stands, and she runs into his open arms. He's a big man with dark-blond hair like mine, and blue eyes like my sister's. His face is open and warm.

Mom edges through the tables toward them. I follow behind with the cake, feeling like a party pooper as I set it carefully on the table.

Dad leans over and kisses Mom on the cheek. "Claire," he says. "You look wonderful."

"No, I don't," she says. But her cheeks flush a little at the compliment.

"And Scarlett." Dad gives me one of his winning smiles. For a second I think that he's going to hold out his hand to shake mine. But then he opens his arms. I stand there, frozen for a second, my mind racing. I could end this whole silly scene right now by refusing to give him a hug. I glance at Mom and my sister. It would ruin their night and poke another pin in my relationship with Mom, like mother-daughter voodoo dolls.

I step forward and let Dad hug me.

The good thing is, I don't have to talk. Mom seems to revive once she's sitting down at the table with a drink in her hand. They chat about the restaurant—when it opened and how it has, in Mom's opinion, the best food in town. She doesn't mention that Em-K proposed to her here. Then Kelsie starts blabbering away, telling Dad every detail of our wedding-dress shopping trip, and all about the filming, including her star singing performance.

"It sounds fantastic, Kels," Dad says. "And I'm so glad you're still such a great singer. Because as it happens, I've got you a little present."

He reaches to the floor behind him and pulls out a big box. Kelsie oohs and ahs, and Mom tuts and says, "oh, you shouldn't have," and Dad replies that "yes, I should—she's my princess." I stare into the flickering candle, hoping he hasn't got me a present too—it's *his* birthday after all, not mine.

Kelsie's present is a brand-new Wii U system with a Disney dance disc, song collection, and microphones. Mom tells her not to, but she still takes everything out of the box, tearing off the plastic wrap, fingering the discs, and getting cords everywhere. The waitress comes over, and Dad orders for us. It's complete chaos, and I'm sure Mom is going to get annoyed at Dad, but instead, she leans toward him and smiles.

"I wasn't sure what to get you, Scarlett," he says.

"What?" I jerk my head around to look at him. "Don't worry. I don't need anything."

He crosses his arms, looking at me like a big, friendly bear. "Now, Scarlett, that wouldn't be fair, would it?"

"It's not my birthday," I say.

He turns to me as Mom is fussing with Kelsie and the Wii stuff that's spread everywhere.

"I'm so sorry I haven't been there for you, Scarlett," he says in a low voice. "And I'm not asking you to accept me overnight—I know that's not going to happen."

"Well..." I so don't want to be having this conversation. "I don't know."

"But maybe," he adds, "we can start to get to know each other better—when you're ready, that is. I find that sometimes, writing things down is easier than saying them in person."

I nod uncomfortably.

"I asked your mom, see, and she said that you have her old laptop. I've read your blog—it's fantastic. We discussed it and decided that it might be time you had an upgrade."

He reaches again behind his chair and pulls out a big, white bag. My heart does a flip. It's from the Apple store.

"No, really..." I say, but my hands betray me and reach out to take the bag.

I pull out a long, thin box. It's a brand-new MacBook Air. My mouth drops open. Mom doesn't even have such a nice computer, and she's been blogging for years now.

"Your mom and I thought this one would be perfect."

I look over at Mom. She nods.

"It is perfect." I press my lips together. "Thank you…Dad."

Dad goes on to ask Mom about the filming and the wedding preparations. The fact that the conversation is so normal makes my skin prickle. It's like everyone's pretending that Dad never left and Mom isn't marrying someone else, and we're all having a nice dinner out on an ordinary Saturday night. It's too weird.

Luckily, the food comes—a big family-size pizza with half pepperoni and extra cheese for Kelsie and me, and half "the works" for Mom and Dad. Mom finally manages to get Kelsie's gift back in the bag, and I put the Apple store bag at my feet, so that it's touching my leg and won't get stolen.

"The pizza looks fantastic," Dad says. "Let's dig in."

The pizza does taste good. Dad launches into an account of his neighbors below his new apartment—and I even find myself laughing once or twice. That's okay, I decide. Just because I'm laughing and enjoying the pizza and the thought of the new computer doesn't mean that I'm back on his side as far as Dad is concerned. But the truth is, I'm tired of being miserable.

In the end, I stop overanalyzing everything, and even start to relax. Although we're all stuffed with pizza, Dad calls the waitress over. She leans in as he hands her the Tupperware with the cake. As she takes it away to the kitchen, he turns to me.

"That was such a nice idea, Scarlett," he says. "And the cake is beautiful—just perfect. I'm so glad you've inherited your mom's thoughtfulness."

"Um, yeah…" I start to laugh, thinking he must be joking. But he's smiling at Mom, and she's smiling at me, and she leans over and pats my hand.

The waitress comes out with the cake on a tray, lit with candles. Following her is what seems like the entire kitchen staff. They begin a rousing chorus of "Happy Birthday" in three-part harmony. Kelsie joins in at the top of her lungs, Mom sings off-key, and I mouth the words. With the cake set before him on the table, Dad takes a deep breath and blows out the candles with a loud bellow. The waiters and even some of the other customers in the restaurant all start to clap, and the waitress snaps a picture of us on Mom's phone.

I don't ask to see the photo, but I can guess what image the camera has caught. The illusion that we're some kind of loving, happy family.

CHAPTER 15

The Dark Side

LATE THAT NIGHT, I SIT on my bed, staring at the white bag from the Apple store. My heart tells me I should go downstairs and give it to Mom—tell her it's not right that I take it. She can work out how to return it to him, or keep it herself—that's up to her. But my head…

I lie back on the pillow and stare at the glow-in-the-dark stars that someone else's dad or mom put up on the ceiling that's now mine. Ever since Dad left, I've tried to be strong—not to think about him or miss him. And for the most part, I've done it. I've tried to be a good daughter, a good sister, a good student, and a good friend. And for the most part, I've done all that too.

And I really have tried to cope with the changes: Mom's

blog, and the damage it caused our relationship, followed by my meeting Mrs. Simpson and then losing her. And then there's the Secret Cooking Club—and all the new experiences, friends, and joy that it's given me—but also the fear that those things could be snatched away. And to top everything off, there's Mom's wedding, the TV thing, my new stepdad-to-be Em-K, and the new life that we're going to have together.

I know I'm lucky—in comparison, my life is amazing and I have so much to be grateful for. In the back of my mind I've always known that, sooner or later, I'd have to come to grips with the "Dad situation," and the hurt it caused me. And I'm not going to be bribed by a new computer or anything else. But if it makes him feel better to give it to me, then who am I to complain?

I take the laptop out of the box and run my hands over its sleek, white lid. Inside, the computer is silver with a black keyboard. I power it up and follow the setup prompts, amazed at how fast and sharp it is, and the fact that it actually belongs to me. It's perfect—and so much more than I ever dreamt of.

The screen prompts me to set up my default email account. I type in my address and password and open the mail icon to access my inbox. There's a "welcome" message that I delete immediately, and one other message.

It's from Dad.

For a second, I hover the cursor over the delete icon. But deep down, I know that's not the right thing to do. I've turned on the computer, personalized it—gone over to the Dark Side. Now, I guess I owe it to Dad to see what he has to say.

I click on the email and read through it.

Dear Scarlett,

I said at dinner that I thought you might find it easier writing to me than talking to me, but the truth is, it's me who finds that easiest. You may not believe it, and I may delete this sentence after I write it because it sounds like a cliché—but the truth is that not a day goes by when I don't think about you and your sister—and your mom—and wish that things might have been different. That I might have been different.

But regrets are not productive, and I'm sure you've heard enough about my excuses and how sorry I am. So, I'm going to draw a line in the sand and pretend that we're starting over, you and I.

I want to be part of your life, Scarlett. No—scratch that—I want to *deserve* to be part of your life. I know that I've got a mountain to climb—and I wish I could say

I was strong enough to do it. But in truth, Scarlett, I'm not very strong or very good—and I think you know that. But I'd like to try. Please, don't delete my emails. Just give me a chance.

Love, Dad

By the time I reach the end, tears are rolling down my cheeks fast and furiously. It's as if the skin has been ripped off my chest and my heart exposed, beating and raw, to the open air. I close the message. I know I should delete it—what business does he have coming back into my life just when things were going in a whole new direction?

But instead, I file it in a new folder that I create: "Dad."

THE SECRET COOKING CLUB

April 24

So this week, a weird thing happened. My real dad turned up wanting to see me—long story—and I ended up making him a birthday cake. It was a chocolate cake, with raspberry jam between the layers. I decorated it with buttercream icing and covered the whole thing with sprinkles. Okay, so it wasn't exactly a classic of cake decorating. But he liked it a lot, and that's the thing that matters most. Now I wonder if maybe he liked it too much...

POST DELETED

April 24

I'm writing this post from my brand-new computer. It's a shiny new Apple, and it's amazing. But the thing is, I've had kind of a weird week, and...

POST DELETED

April 24

Sorry for the quick post today—I've got lots of homework! I've found a fantastic recipe for spring fondant fancies. I'll post it soon! If you give it a try, make sure you post a photo. Off to do some more grammar now (yawn)! But first, I'm going downstairs to make myself a nice cup of hot chocolate with cinnamon and sprinkles on top.

The Little Cook

xx

CHAPTER 16

The Next Level

"HOW DID THE CAKE TURN out?"

My pulse jolts as Nick comes up to me on my way to class. His hand brushes mine—I'm not sure whether or not he meant it to—but either way, my skin tingles.

"Good." I come to a stop. People push past us in the crowded hall. I cock my head. "Maybe too good."

Nick nods. I'm pretty sure he gets my whole dilemma. "Did you take a photo for the Instagram page?"

I take out my phone and show him the photo snapped by the waitress—Mom emailed it to me this morning. His eyes widen.

"Ah," he says. "Maybe it was too good." He looks up at me. "Your hair looks nice, though."

"Thanks." I try to hide my blush. "The whole evening

was really weird. No—scratch that—my whole life is weird these days."

"Well, maybe things would be better if you came back to the club. It might help to get away from the wedding stuff." He glances down at the phone in my hand with the photo on the screen. "There is still going to be a wedding, right?"

"Yeah, 'fraid so." I tell him about the day spent at the awful posh boutiques and then the Bridal Center. I'm expecting him to sympathize with me, but instead he laughs. "You have to let all of us know when it's going to be on TV," he says. "We so have to get together to watch it."

"I definitely won't be watching it," I grumble. "And I can name at least two other people who won't be watching either." I flick my head down the hall to where Gretchen has just arrived with Alison. Gretchen looks at me, puts up her hand and whispers something to Alison. I feel a pang in my stomach. How could things have gone so wrong? "And those same people won't want me back in the club either."

"You're so wrong, Scarlett." Nick shakes his head. "I just don't get you and Gretchen—I mean, you two are so alike."

"Alike—no! You must be nuts."

He laughs. "Neither of you see it. Maybe that's your problem."

The bell rings. "Anyway," he adds, "there was talk of meeting up after school. Come and join us."

Okay—I'll be there! I feel like shouting.

"I'll think about it," I say. With a shrug, I turn and walk away.

I'll think about it. It's like somehow Gretchen has taken over my body and her words are coming out of my mouth. Could Nick possibly be right? I mean, Gretchen is stubborn, proud, and opinionated, and she knows how to stand up for what she believes in. If anything, I wish I could be more like her.

As the teacher writes our math assignment up on the board, I wonder what I would think if I were Gretchen and she were me. Would I see "me" as stuck up, trying to hog all the limelight just because my mom has some kind of B-list celebrity complex? I guess it's possible. Even though it's completely wrong.

But I've misunderstood Gretchen in the past too. Once, I thought she was ignoring me because of Mom's blog, but it turned out I was wrong—she thought it was me who was acting stuck up. Either way, Nick said they would have me back in the club if I wanted to. And I *seriously* want to.

I pack away my notebook and steel myself to try to catch Gretchen between classes. Because if there's one thing I've learned over all these months, it's that my life is always a lot better with the Secret Cooking Club in it.

Just before lunch, I get a text message from Annie—the assistant to Producer Poppy. She wants me to call and set up a time to come in to the studio and be filmed making the wedding cake. Just reading the message, I feel the familiar wave of nausea at the idea of being in front of a camera. I'm about to delete the message when out of the corner of my eye, I see Gretchen coming out of the girls' bathroom—alone, for once. I shove my phone in my pocket and walk quickly toward her before I can chicken out.

"Gretchen?" I say.

She stops and turns around.

"Do you have a quick sec?"

"Okay." There's wariness in her voice. "Your hair looks good."

"Thanks." I pull her off to the side as kids swarm by on their way to the cafeteria for lunch. But as soon as we're alone, my confidence drains away. Gretchen puts her hands on her hips, not cutting me any slack.

"I'm sorry," I say. "For what I said before, and for walking out. It's just...I don't know...things are really stressful right now. I guess I didn't really think."

Gretchen stares at me, but her face seems to soften a little bit. "I know you do lots with the club and the blog, Scarlett," she says. "And you deserve the recognition you get. But sometimes, I think you forget that the rest of us want to help too."

I hang my head. "I know. And it's so unnecessary. It's just, there's a part of me that misses the way it was. When it was just us—you know? Cooking in Rosemary's kitchen. Trying new things. Doing it for fun…" I sigh. "And when it was still our secret."

She nods slowly. "I know what you mean," she says. "But it was never going to stay that way. We took the club to the next level and made it something that lots of kids could do. And now, maybe this TV thing is taking it even further. But I think you need to decide—if it's you, or *us*."

"I know. And I have decided. This was never something I wanted. I know I need to talk to the producer woman, but I'm just so bad at these things."

She laughs. "No you're not. I mean, you're 'The Little Cook.' You need to tell them what you want to do."

I roll my eyes. For Gretchen, talking to adults is easy-peasy. But not for me.

"Come up with a plan. Then pitch it to them." She makes it sound so obvious.

"A plan? Like what?"

"I don't know. But we can talk about it. We're meeting up today after school. Can you make it?"

"Yeah." I start to feel a little bit better.

"Good. We were going to meet at Alison's house—unless you think we can use Rosemary's kitchen?"

"We can—I'm sure. In fact, the wall's been knocked through between our two houses."

"Really?" Gretchen raises an eyebrow.

"They're supposed to be putting in a door, but it hasn't happened yet."

"Okay," she says. "I'll let the others know."

As Gretchen walks away down the hallway, I feel like we're two sides of the same person, who have somehow managed to bungle each other's lines.

Violet rushes up to me after lessons. "OMG, it's true, right? You're back?" She throws her arms around me in a bear hug.

"I'm back." I breathe in the smell of her apple shampoo, feeling better than I have in days. I don't dwell on the little niggling thought that she sort of chose the others over me.

"That's fab," she says, smiling like her old self. "We've missed you."

"I missed you too," I say. "What are you making today?"

"Something for the school cafeteria, I think." She looks unsure. "Gretchen's kind of been running the show. Though Naya's got good ideas too—and she's not afraid to give her opinion. And I've been busy with these…" She fumbles in her bag. "Here, look."

She takes out a sketchbook and flips forward a few pages. I look over her shoulder, my eyes widening in amazement.

"You drew these?" I stare at the sketches she's made on the page. Layer cakes and braided breads, fruit tarts and cupcakes. The drawings—done in pen, filled in with colored pencil—look good enough to eat. She's written out the recipes, labeled the ingredients, and drawn little arrows saying what goes where.

She nods. "Do you like them?"

"They look amazing."

Violet beams. "Do you really think so?"

"I know so. When did you have time to do them?"

Her face clouds for a moment—or maybe it's my imagination. "I did most of them late at night. I've kind of been having trouble sleeping—"

My phone buzzes in my pocket with a text message. I quickly check the screen—it's Mom, asking me if I've spoken with the assistant producer yet. I shove the phone back in my pocket as an idea suddenly strikes me. I look down at Violet's sketches again just as she closes the notebook and puts it back in her bag.

"Hold that thought and let me make a phone call," I say to her. "But I'll see you later—okay?"

CHAPTER 17

A Summer Fête

AFTER SCHOOL, I GO STRAIGHT home and dump my bag. As I go through the hole in the wall, I wonder when the door will be put in. Mom's too busy and preoccupied to be bothered about it, and I suppose it makes sense to wait until after the wedding—in case something goes wrong. Not that it will...

Treacle eyes me warily from his basket as I cut up some trash bags and tack them over the jagged edges of bricks and plaster that have been knocked through. "It's like a great big cat flap," I explain to him. He swishes his tail like I'm not making any sense. But I know what I'm doing. I don't want Mom catching a glimpse of what we might be getting up to—once I explain my idea to the others, that is.

I've just managed to cover most of the opening when the others begin to arrive: first, Gretchen, Alison, and Nick; then

Violet's "crush," Fraser, then Naya. I pass around a plate of homemade dark chocolate and orange cookies that were made by Nick and Fraser, while we wait for Violet (who had to stop off home before coming here). When Violet finally arrives, I poke my head back through the flap of trash bags and make sure that Mom's nowhere to be seen. Just like Violet said, when I come back to the others, Gretchen has already taken charge.

"So," she says, "what shall we make today? Does anyone have any ideas, or new recipes to try?"

Naya and Violet both shoot up their hands. Naya's brought a recipe for tomato, spinach, and cheese tartlets that she and Alison want to try. Violet takes out her sketchbook and shows them a drawing she made of some white chocolate and cranberry muffins drizzled with royal icing and demerara sugar.

"Your drawings are so amazing, Violet," Gretchen says. "If we have all the ingredients, we can make both."

Nick and Naya go to check the cupboards. I sit at the table and tentatively raise my hand.

"Yes, Scarlett," Gretchen says, sounding like a principal. "By the way, welcome back."

"Thanks," I say. "Um, I don't want to speak out of turn, but I…um…had an idea. I want to run it by you." I look at Gretchen, then at the others. "All of you."

"Go on, then," Nick encourages.

"Well, it's about Mom's wedding. You know? And the TV show she's doing." I seem to swallow the words. I can't look at Gretchen.

"Yeah?" Violet says. "They're going to film you doing the cake, right?"

"Right. But actually, I had another thought." I lower my voice in case Mom has somehow managed to enter our kitchen without my hearing. "It's not definite yet, but I had a quick chat earlier with the assistant TV producer. Her name's Annie. She seems nice."

"So what's the idea?" Alison prompts.

"Well, the TV station is paying for different bits of the wedding—like the cake and the food. They were going to get some fancy caterers to do the food—canapés, main courses, desserts—all that stuff. But I was thinking…" I take a breath, "that we could all do it—together."

"Really?" Violet says. "They'll buy us everything we need?"

"Shh." I point to the thin layer of trash bags covering the hole in the wall. "I thought it could be the Secret Cooking Club's big secret. Mom can't find out. I don't even want the main producer of the show—some loud woman called Poppy that I met over the weekend—to know. Not yet, at least."

Gretchen puts her hands on her hips. "What exactly are you suggesting?"

"That you could be on TV too!" I say. "We all could—those of you that want to. I mean, think how great it would be. We could do an amazing menu, and Violet could do the drawings, just like the artist on *Bake Off*."

Violet's face shines. "OMG, I'd love to do that."

"So this would be part of the bride show?" Naya asks.

"Yeah—it's about brides preparing for their special day. It totally fits. But like Violet said before, any old bride can get food done by caterers. But not every bride can have a wedding feast made by the Secret Cooking Club."

"I like it," Gretchen says. "If you think you can pull it off."

"And what about the menu?" Alison asks.

"I know you've all be collecting recipes," I say. "We could put something together, and I'll give it to Annie at the TV station. She can show it to Mom. That's what the caterers would do, I think."

"I could do the starters," Fraser says. "Something with smoked salmon. I've been to all my cousins' weddings, and they always have that."

"Smoked salmon is good," Naya says. "But we should probably have a theme. It's a summer wedding, isn't it?"

I take a deep breath and drop the bomb. "Actually, it's early summer. It's supposed to happen in eight weeks!"

"Eight weeks!" Naya looks shocked. "That's ridiculous."

"Yeah," I say. "It is."

Gretchen frowns. "We'd better get on it, then. Violet, do you have your notebook?"

Everybody starts talking at once. If Mom did happen to be listening from our kitchen, the cat would be out of the bag already.

"Shh," I say, pointing at the hole in the wall. "We need to keep it secret. Violet, do you want to write down everyone's suggestions?"

"Sure." She opens her little book to a blank page and sharpens a pencil. "Go ahead."

"What about bite-sized strawberry tarts with crème fraîche?" Alison suggests immediately. "The strawberries will be in season in June."

"What about going with a color theme?" Violet says. "Like, we could do a salad with edible flowers and shaved Parmesan. I also found a recipe for lavender salad cream."

"Or we could do it by cuisine," Naya says. "French or Italian. Or sushi rolls—that's a big thing at weddings, I think."

"Yeah, it is," Violet says. "And what about those volley-something-or-other things that your mom wanted? The fancy sausage rolls?"

"Vol-au-vents!" I say.

"That's it!"

Again, everyone starts talking at once. There are so many ideas floating around, but no rhyme or reason to anything. The phrase "too many cooks spoil the broth" pops into my head.

Eventually, I tap the table. "Okay, that's great, everyone," I say loudly. "That's given us lots to think about. But—"

"Did you see this?" I look up at Nick, who's standing by the counter. In front of him is *The Little Cook*, the special handwritten recipe book that we use. I've read the whole book over and over, cover to cover. But now Nick is pointing to a page that I swear I've never seen before. Maybe the pages were stuck together, or maybe there's just something a little strange that goes on sometimes in Rosemary's kitchen.

"It's a menu for a 'Summer Fête,'" he says.

"Really? You mean like a summer fair?"

"Or a party, I think." Nick hands Violet the book, and she passes it down the table to me.

In my hands, the little book seems warm, like a loaf of bread that's come out of the oven. I read over the menu, handwritten with little flowers drawn down the side, and a colored-pencil sketch of some children dancing around a maypole. Then I pass the book back down the table so that everyone can see. There's a new energy in the air, a new spark to our meeting.

Violet looks at me, her eyes shining. She's aware of it too. For the first time in a while, it's like I can't stop smiling.

"It's perfect," I say. "Let's do it."

"A Summer Fête"

Drinks
Sparkling raspberry and lavender lemonade
Miniature vanilla and strawberry milkshakes

First Course
Smoked salmon and cream cheese pancakes
Pea and mint soup with cream garnish (v)

Second Course
Organic herb-roasted chicken with wild mushrooms
—or—
Medallions of fillet steak in peppercorn sauce
—or—
Spring vegetable risotto (v)
with garlic and herb potatoes and fresh vegetables

Dessert
Assorted tea biscuits
Salted caramel and dark chocolate truffles
Wedding cake

CHAPTER 18

Our New Secret

"DO YOU THINK WE COULD keep it a secret? From…you know… Mom?" While the others are still chatting about the menu, I've given Assistant Annie a quick call. Since Mom's allowing the TV station to be in charge of the catering, there's no point in getting excited over our menu unless they're on board.

"I think it sounds like a fantastic idea," Assistant Annie says. "Of course, I'll need to get it signed off with my boss— and you're sure you can really do it?"

I look down the length of Rosemary's kitchen. Gretchen has grabbed an armload of cookbooks from the shelf and is passing them out. The Little Cook didn't have recipes for all the things on the menu, but I'm willing to bet that Rosemary Simpson marked them in her other cookbooks. Once we find the recipes, we'll have to practice each of the dishes—make sure we know exactly what we're doing. Then we can decide if we want to make some changes to add our own twist to the recipes—like vol-au-vents. It's all going to take time and a lot of effort.

"I know we can," I say. Because now that the Secret Cooking Club is on the case, I feel like things are right back on track.

I end the call and return to my friends. "It's a thumbs-up!" I say.

"Great," Gretchen says, barely looking up from the recipe book she's flipping through.

"I've found two of the recipes," Naya says, looking excited. "For the salted caramel truffles and the spring vegetable risotto." She skims the recipe. "It looks like it's some special kind of rice with vegetables."

"Cool," Nick says. He looks over at me. "Should I try making it? We can have it for dinner."

Violet and I glance at each other. I'm not sure that rice with vegetables sounds particularly appetizing, but one thing I've learned since starting the Secret Cooking Club is to be brave and try new things. Most of the time—when we're using our special recipes, at least—even things that don't sound too good on paper turn out to be delicious.

"I'll help," Alison says. The two of them get up and go over to the larder where the fresh vegetables are stored.

"Should we try the truffles?" I look at Violet. Her head turns in Fraser's direction. "Fraser, do you want to help?" I ask.

"Um, sure." He gets up from the table. I'm hoping that Violet doesn't notice his quick glance at Alison.

"Great," I say.

"I'll keep looking for the recipes," Naya says. "Then maybe we can whip up some muffins for school?" She glances at Gretchen. "Okay?"

"Sure," Gretchen says. "I'll give you a hand."

With everything agreed, I get up from the table, determined to "keep out of the way" of Violet and Fraser. But Violet seems to be overcome by an attack of shyness. "Um, what should I do?" she asks.

"You and Fraser melt the caster sugar," I direct. I open the cupboard and hand her the packet of sugar.

"Okay, Fraser, can you get the pan out?"

Leaving the two of them to work, I find the other ingredients and set them out. She and Fraser seem a little awkward together. He measures out the sugar while Violet heats the pan. Once he tips it in, she swirls the hot sugar toward the middle so that it dissolves evenly. I bring her some vanilla, staring into the pan as the mixture gradually turns a dark, golden-brown color.

Violet measures out the vanilla and sea salt and tips them in. "I'm just so glad you're back," she says to me. "I missed this. I mean, it's like old times, isn't it?"

I nod, knowing what she means. At the beginning, it was just her and me, trying to puzzle our way through the lists of ingredients and the many steps of instructions. We made cinnamon scones, and then caramel flapjacks. Those went well, so we got more confident and tried more complicated things like banoffee pie. Then, we learned to cook real food—eggs, meat, vegetables. Once, we even did a whole four-course dinner.

"Are you ready for the brown sugar and cream?" Fraser steps over, and I move away to get some chilled butter out of the fridge.

"It smells so good," I hear Violet say.

"Yeah," Fraser says.

I bring over the butter and then go to break up the dark chocolate into a bowl. Naya and Gretchen are laughing as they make the muffins—somehow Naya has managed to get her black hair completely dusted with flour like an old-fashioned powdered wig. I feel a little stab of pride that all these people who might never have known each other, and who probably wouldn't have been friends, have come together here in this very special kitchen.

When Violet and Fraser have added the butter and the rest of the cream, I pour the mixture over the dark chocolate. It looks and smells heavenly. I take the bowl to the fridge to cool.

Nick and Alison have finished chopping the vegetables and are preparing to cook the rice.

I go back to the table, noticing that Gretchen and Naya have used up nearly half a pack of yellow Post-its marking pages in the various cookbooks. Suddenly, I have an attack of nerves. This is by far the biggest project the Secret Cooking Club has taken on since our first online bake-a-thon where we raised money for a charity for the elderly.

Gretchen sees me standing there and comes over. "It's going to be a big job," she says, like she's reading my mind.

I keep my voice low. "Do you think we're up to it?"

She looks around at all the others: stirring, chopping, washing up; laughing, chatting, and working together.

"I hope so," she says. We both smile.

THE SECRET COOKING CLUB

April 25: Special Bulletin

Help! I'm looking for a few volunteers to come and help us with a very special project. Details and venue to follow. I promise, there will be lots of great food for everyone to enjoy.

The Little Cook

xx

CHAPTER 19

Another "Truth"

LATER THAT EVENING, I HIT post and the bulletin is posted to the website. I don't know for sure that it will work, but other Secret Cooking Club "flash mobs" have worked before, according to the stories that other members have posted on the website. I'm not quite sure how the TV station is going to handle a huge group of kids cooking together in their studio, but I do know that we'll need all the help we can get, and it will be fun for as many members as possible of the cyber club to be involved. At least there will be plenty of grown-ups around to "supervise" us. I just hope I can count on Assistant Annie to make it all happen.

I close the blog and pop a truffle into my mouth, savoring the soft, oozy caramel. Dusted in cocoa powder with a tiny crystallized violet on top, the truffles turned out well, if a little too big. That's the thing I've discovered about cooking—it always helps to try a recipe more than once because sometimes things don't go according to plan. Just like life, I guess.

I check out some of the stories and photos that have been posted recently on the blog. It's incredible how many creative, beautiful, and fun things people have made. There's a volcano cake with a river of red licorice spewing out like lava—made by a ten-year-old boy member named Thomas. There's a batch of sparkly butterfly fairy cakes that a thirteen-year-old made for her little sister's birthday. Another girl posted a homemade pizza with fresh tomato sauce and sausage, absolutely dripping with mozzarella cheese. A group of kids from a school in another state are holding a charity bake-off at a local children's center. We also have six new followers.

And there's one photo in particular that grabs my attention. It's a batch of heart-shaped cookies with pink and purple piping, glitter, sprinkles, and Smarties all at the same time. The photo caption reads: I made these for my brother's birthday. Hope you like them. Love, Annabel Greene.

Annabel Greene. At first it takes me a second to remember the name. She was the winner of the school bake-off I did before the Easter holiday. I'm so glad that she's joined the online club! I "like" her photo and add a comment: Those are so beautiful. You have a real talent. Scarlett x.

When I've finished looking at the member page, I upload the photos I've taken tonight of the truffles, and the risotto, which—though it was strictly speaking rice with vegetables—was tasty and warming. If Mom sees the post and asks me about the "special project," I'll tell her that we're doing a summer lunch at the old people's home. Though recently, Mom's been way too busy to do much lurking on my blog.

All in all, I feel happy that I've patched things up with my friends, and that we've got a new secret project to work on. And glad that Annabel Greene has kept up with her baking. But as I shut down the website, the good thoughts vanish. There's a little stamp icon at the bottom of the screen with a tiny red number "1" over it. One new message.

If only I hadn't opened the bag from the Apple store and the box inside. I knew in my heart that I should have returned the gift—why didn't I? Did I really need a new computer that badly? Creating a little hole for a worm of unhappiness to creep into my room, and my mind. Maybe I should tell Mom about the emails—get her to tell *him* to leave me alone. Maybe…

There's nothing to do about it. I won't be able to go to

sleep until I've faced it. Swallowing hard, I click on the mail icon and open the message.

Dear Scarlett,

Me again. You haven't responded—and that's fine. I said I wasn't going to talk about the past, but there are a few things on the record that maybe I need to set straight. So, I've decided to lay it all on the line, and let you decide for yourself.

First, I should tell you why I left. Things weren't going so well between your mom and me—I was stressed out at work and I didn't find it easy to talk to her about how I felt. I want you to know that it wasn't your mom's fault, or your fault, or your sister's fault. It happened, and there's nothing I can say or do to change that or take away that hurt.

I know this might not do anything to help things between us, but I wanted to make sure that you knew the truth.

Love, Dad

The truth. I read the message several times, trying to take in everything that the words say and don't say. He's right that it doesn't help. But as I file it away in the "Dad" folder, somehow it feels like a chapter is closing behind me. A few questions have been answered and no longer have to haunt me. I shut down the computer and lie on the bed, staring at the stars on the ceiling until I finally drop off to sleep.

CHAPTER 20

A Drizzle
of Suspicion

THE NEXT WEEK GOES BY in a blur. I gather some recipes for the tiers of the wedding cake, and try a few at home. Mom is wrapped up in a flurry of fittings and invitations and coffees with friends—something Mom usually never makes time to do. Once or twice, when I overhear her making plans, I have a nagging suspicion that at least one of the "friends" is actually Dad. Not that she can't meet up with him if she wants—I mean, they aren't married anymore so I guess they can be friends. I'm sure they have lots to catch up on for "old times' sake." Though it seems weird that she'd want to see him now, of all times.

Em-K is away for a few days, and whenever I hear Mom speaking to him on the phone, they seem to be arguing—something I haven't heard them do before. When that happens, I stick in my earbuds, turn on some music, and try not to listen.

The good news is that things are going much better at school. At break time and lunchtime, the known members of the Secret Cooking Club gather to discuss the menu, the recipes, and life in general. We've added a few twists of our own to the menu—sausage rolls in puff pastry, sushi and cucumber rolls, rainbow fruit kebabs, and vegetarian lasagna. I've also got a few responses to the message I put out to the wider world. It makes me feel good to know that the kids who have joined the club online are actually real people. And there's one response that makes me really happy. At lunchtime, I read it aloud to Gretchen, Violet, and Naya, who are sitting at my table in the cafeteria.

Hi, Scarlett. Thanks for liking my photo. You may not remember me, but we met when you judged the bake-off at my school. I just wanted to say thanks for picking me as star baker, because I'm new at my school, and I was finding it hard to make friends. After the bake-off, I met two other girls who like to bake, and now things are so much better. I wanted to email before, but I was kind of scared. But if you really do want people to come and help you for the special project, my mom says she'll let me do it. Thanks again, so much.

Love, Annabel Greene

"That's so sweet," Violet says. "She sounds nice."

Gretchen takes out the pages of lists she's been making of people, dishes on the menu, ingredients, and practice times—she's taken to her role as organizer like a duck to water.

"Should I add her to main dishes, or do you want her for starters?" she asks Naya.

"I'll gladly have her," Naya says.

"I could do with someone else on desserts too," Violet says. "The cake we're planning has six tiers."

"Okay," Gretchen says. "I'll add her there too."

"Maybe we should ask her what she wants to do," I throw out.

But luckily I don't have to brave Gretchen's response because just then, the bell rings—lunch is over. As I'm about to silence my phone, I accidentally scroll down from Annabel Greene's message and catch sight of the folder marked "Dad." Instantly, I feel like a rain cloud has come in through the open window and made a beeline for my head.

The four of us leave the cafeteria. As we pass the office, I notice there's a new bulletin board up, with the caption: "Don't let the worry monsters drag you down!" There are some furry monsters peeking out of a zippered bag tacked to the board. The board then lists all the people you can talk to if you feel worried: a teacher, a school counselor, a good friend. For a second, I wonder what it would be like to get the heavy bag of worries off my back.

"How ridiculous." Gretchen rolls her eyes at the board.

I look away, feeling silly that I took it seriously.

Naya and Gretchen go off to science. Violet and I both have PE. Just outside the changing rooms, I slow down and pull her aside. "Can I talk to you for a sec?" I say.

"Sure." She narrows her eyes. "Are you okay? What's up?"

"Sorry. It's just…" I hesitate, finding it hard to share my worries, even with my best friend. "You have to swear not to tell any of the others," I say.

She crosses her arms. "You know you can trust me—don't you?"

"Yeah, but—"

"Is this about Nick?" she interrupts, loud enough for half the school to hear.

"No. Shhh…" I pull her closer and lean in toward her blue-black hair. "It's just that…well…my dad is kind of like…back."

As the other girls file past us into the changing room, I tell her everything. From Mom running into Dad at the TV station, to the dinner, the new computer, and the emails. "I think she's also had coffee with him a few times," I say.

Violet looks thoughtful. "Maybe they're just catching up."

"They can do that on the phone, surely."

"I don't know—it might not be a bad thing if they're friends. Especially if he's back in town."

"But that's just it. Dad has been totally *out* of our lives for so long. It all just feels really weird that he's back. And now, of all times."

"Maybe. But your Mom loves Em-K, right?" Violet's voice rises. "You know how we all thought they were a weird couple at first. But now, it just seems normal that they're together."

It's true that for a long time after Mom and Em-K got together, none of us really "got it." I mean, he's a congressman—why would he want to be with someone like Mom? It's not like it was going to help his political career to be dating a mommy blogger with two kids.

But that's one of the things that, over time, I've learned to like most about Em-K. He's not just in politics for his image.

He really does care about trying to make things better, and he's a real person underneath. If he's with Mom, it's because he loves her and wants to be with her—and us. The problem is, can I say the same about Mom?

I rub at my head that's starting to ache from the whole thing.

"They're arguing a lot too," I say. "Just like Mom and Dad used to do."

"Well, I'm sure the wedding and the TV thing are stressful. But your mom seems to really want this wedding."

"Yeah, she does. But Em-K wasn't too happy about the TV thing, and the rush to do the wedding in two months. But he went along with it. Then Dad turned up out of the blue, and things got worse." I stare down at the grimy tiled floor of the corridor. "I just want things to be settled. And for this wedding to go ahead, and then be over. I'm scared that something's going to go wrong."

"I'm sorry, Scarlett…" Violet makes like she's going to hug me, but my phone vibrates in my pocket. An incoming call.

I fish the phone out and check the screen. It's a number I don't recognize and instantly, I'm wary—could it be Dad calling from a landline? I let it go to voicemail, then dial in and listen to the message. It's not from Dad, but rather from Producer Poppy, the boss of Assistant Annie.

Scarlett! I hope you don't mind my calling you direct. My assistant told me your idea about the secret club—lovely! But I'm afraid it's too much for the station to take on at such short notice. So let's focus on getting you here to make the cake. We've got a kitchen in the studio for our celebrity chefs that will knock your socks off. Call me, okay?

The message ends. My stomach tightens in a knot. I pass the phone to Violet, and she listens to the message. Other than a tiny flash of disappointment, she doesn't react and hands me back the phone.

"Don't worry." She smiles reassuringly. "You tried. Gretchen knows that. And we can still do the menu—maybe we can do a summer lunch at the old people's home."

"No…" The word comes out of my mouth sounding tortured.

"Hey! It's cool. You'll be a star. You're going to have your very own celebrity kitchen and your own show."

"But, Violet," I whisper, "I don't want any of those things. I just want to be part of the Secret Cooking Club."

She shrugs. "Okay. But just remember, most people would love to be in your position."

"I'll tell you a secret," I say. More than anything, I *must* make her understand. "I know it sounds totally silly, but when we were in that bridal shop, and the cameras and the spotlights were on me, I felt sick—like my lunch was going to come up all over the dry-clean-only dresses. It was awful. And I've had it before—when I speak in front of assembly at the charity bake-offs. It's the same feeling I had back when I was counting down the minutes till one of Mom's blog posts. I think maybe there's something wrong with me."

Violet cocks her head. "You had stage fright. It can happen any time—like where your adrenaline kicks in and you feel out of control."

"I certainly felt out of control."

"My aunt Hilda says she feels that way sometimes when she's meeting clients. She's a real estate agent, so she has to show strangers around houses and talk to them on the phone and stuff."

"So what does she do?"

"Yoga and meditation—stuff like that."

I roll my eyes. "You think doing yoga is going to help me go on TV in front of millions of people, annoy all my friends, and cook something in a celebrity chef kitchen without my voice going hoarse and my hands shaking as I'm trying to measure out a teaspoon of salt?"

"Well, if it's as bad as you say, then maybe yoga is worth a try."

"No! What's worth a try is calling Producer Poppy back. Maybe Annie didn't explain it right. How fantastic it's going to be. And if she still insists that it's just me, then I'll tell her I can't do it. That…I don't want to do it."

"Okay, okay, I've got it."

"Good." I breathe out.

"Here's what we'll do," Violet says. "Let's meet up after school. I've got something I need to do right after." Her eyes grow dark, like it's something she's dreading. "I can come to your house about five. You can call her back, and I'll be there so I can let you know how you did. Is that a deal?"

"It's a deal." I suddenly notice how quiet it is around us. "We'd better go in and get changed." I pull a face. More than once, Violet and I have been late to PE because we were chatting and had to do ten push-ups each as a punishment.

Sure enough, we're the last ones to get changed. As I'm shoving my school clothes in the locker and starting to put on my gym uniform, I realize how, once again, the entire conversation has been about me and my problems. Why can't I be a better friend?

"What about you?" I say. "How are things going with Fraser?" I keep my voice low in case anyone's still in the bathroom—I know Violet would be mortified if it got spread around that she liked him. "You guys seemed pretty cozy making the truffles the other day."

"Oh that." Maybe it's her slouchy gym top, but Violet's shoulders seem to slump. "I don't know," she says. "He hasn't texted me in the last day or so. I guess it's pretty hopeless."

"Hey, don't say that." Talking about someone else's problems, I'm on more solid ground. "He seems a little shy. You have to work out how to get him to come out of his shell."

We sit side by side on the bench and put on our sneakers.

"I...I don't know. I just wish..." All of a sudden, the sadness I've noticed in Violet recently seems to be back in force. "Maybe it isn't a good time—for either of us."

"Look." I grab her hand and pull her off the bench. She's helped me by listening, so the least I can do is help her with her boy troubles. "Let's kill two birds with one stone. When we meet up later, I'll make my phone call, and then we'll make something for Fraser."

"Make something?"

"You know, like we talked about—we'll bake him something for you to give him. Like a 'welcome to the club' gift, or something."

She cocks her head sideways. "He's not the only new member. There's Naya too..."

"I know, but come on, Violet—you have to do something. I thought we could make him something Scottish—like short-bread cookies. That's Scottish, isn't it?"

Her face flushes. "I don't know."

"Well, let's pretend we know. We'll come up with a cool flavor, and you can pipe chocolate on the top. Fraser likes chocolate."

Her eyes brighten. "Yes, he does."

"So...you're in?"

From inside the gym, a whistle blows. Late again—my arms are already aching from the thought of the push-ups.

"I'm in," she says. We both take off at a run to join the class.

CHAPTER 21

The Worry Monsters

THINGS MAY NOT BE sorted—far from it. But at least we have a plan. When I get home, I go to the kitchen to get a snack. Immediately the door to the Mom Cave slams. "You know how important this is to me!" Mom is yelling into the phone. I don't hear the response, but then she says, "Well, if you don't like it, then don't turn up on the day!"

I wince, wishing I hadn't overheard. Surely, Mom can't be talking like that to Em-K—as in, the man she's going to marry? They've been fighting a lot lately, but like Violet said, that's just wedding nerves—it must be!

Inside the Mom Cave, things seem to quieten down— one of them must have put down the phone. I expect her to come out at any second, though I'm not quite sure what to say if she does. She won't be happy that I haven't sorted out things with the TV producer—quite the opposite. Now that Producer Poppy has ditched my brilliant idea, I feel like telling her that I won't do the show at all. That will drive Mom nuts. And even if I did do the show, Mom won't want any advice from me—like that maybe she should be a little bit nicer to her husband-to-be. She may not write her tell-all parenting blog anymore, but when it comes to relationships, she sees herself as the expert.

Still, she's my mom, and if she's upset, I should try to help. I'm about to go knock on the door and offer her a cup of tea when I hear her voice again—this time lower. "Oh, hi. Hope this isn't a bad time. I just...thought maybe we could meet up for a drink. I could use one." There's a pause and then she laughs—a high-pitched laughter that I don't remember hearing before. It's not a good sound.

But before I can listen in any further, the doorbell rings. Relieved at the distraction, I go to answer it. It's Violet. I take one look at her face, and know that something bad has happened.

"What's the matter?" I say, alarmed.

"Nothing." She looks down at the mat. "I'm fine."

Two hours ago, when lessons ended for the day, she was fine. I went home, and she said she had something to do right after school. I don't know where she went, but now she most definitely is *not* fine.

"Come on in." I usher her. "Do you want some cake? I made one the other day to practice for the wedding cake—it's raspberry ripple with white chocolate icing."

She shakes her head. "I'm not hungry."

If I didn't already guess that something is majorly wrong, this confirms it. If anyone has a sweet tooth, it's Violet.

"Okay." I lead her inside past the front room where Kelsie's watching TV, into our kitchen, and through the wall to Rosemary's kitchen. The huge stove that always gives off a little heat makes the room cozy and comforting. But today, it's as if neither of us even notice.

"Sit," I command. I go to the fridge and get out a jug of orange juice. I pour two glasses and sit opposite her. She takes the glass and stares at it without blinking.

"I hope this isn't about Fraser," I say. "Because we're going to get that sorted out. I found a recipe for butter short-bread with cranberry and orange. Doesn't that sound good? With chocolate piped over the top…" I trail off, feeling like I'm pleading for a lost cause.

"I think…" She bites her lip and turns away.

"Violet!" I come over to her side of the table and try to

put my arm around her shoulder, but she shrugs me off. I've seen her upset before—when we've had a falling-out, when she's argued with Aunt Hilda—and, whether she admits it or not, over the whole Fraser thing. But there's something about seeing her like this…well, it scares me.

"Hey," I say softly, sitting in the chair next to her. "Whatever it is, you know you can talk about it with me. You're my best friend."

"I don't want to talk about it," she says. "I've done enough of that."

"But it's not Fraser—"

"No," she snaps, jumping up from the chair. "It's not Fraser or any foolish…boy crush thing."

I stare up at her like she's struck me. "Okay, fine, if you don't want to tell me—"

"I've been seeing a counselor," she blurts out. "After school. That's why I couldn't come right away."

"A counselor?" I blink. Violet's such a fun, happy person—so normal. "I thought they were for kids with…" I say without thinking. I can't finish the sentence. Of course, she's seeing a counselor—she lost her parents! I must be dense for not realizing it before.

"With what?" Violet stares at me. "Mental problems?"

"I was going to say 'problems,'" I lie, knowing she's hit the nail on the head.

"Problems." Her laugh is bitter and hollow. "If that's what it's about, then half the kids at school would need to do it—wouldn't they? Or even all of them."

"Maybe."

"Well, I talked to the counselor because I don't want my friends to think I'm some kind of freak."

"I would never think that! You can talk to me. I mean…" I pause, ashamed. "I'm constantly going on about my issues."

"It just sounds foolish when I talk about it. But it's really messing with my head. I'm not sleeping, and I keep having nightmares." She purses her lips. "About my parents."

"Oh." The room suddenly seems chilly. I rewind back to the first few days and weeks when I met Violet. She was new at our school, and I thought we could be friends because she didn't know about all the baggage I was carrying with Mom's blog. One day, I'd been whining and moaning about Mom and the blog and how bad I felt…Me, me, me. Violet was living with her aunt Hilda, and before that day, I'd never asked why.

When she told me—that both of her parents had been killed in a car accident—I couldn't believe it at first. But I soon got the whole story, and all the awful details. Her dad had been killed outright, but her mom was in a coma for months before she died. I still can't even imagine how it must have been for her. I mean—I've got my issues with both my mom and my dad. But I just don't know how I could ever handle it if I lost both of them like that.

"I keep dreaming about the house where we lived," she continues. "It's so real…"

"And what happens in the dream?"

"My parents are there in the house. It's like they aren't…" she takes a breath, "…dead." The word echoes around the room, seeming to suck the air away. "It's like they're living there, going about their lives, and I'm not there with them. It's like…I'm the one who's gone."

I shiver. "What does the counselor say?"

She sinks back against the counter, looking at the floor. For a second, I worry she's not going to answer; that even talking about it is proving to be too much.

"She says I need 'closure,'" she says, finally breaking the silence. "That's what they call it. It's like, closing a door on the past, so that I can move on. I've never really accepted that they're gone. That they're not coming back. And for some reason, I've tangled things up in my mind that they might still be at our old house living our old life."

I don't know what to say, but I move closer to her.

"Which just sounds so…silly. I mean, I *know* they're dead—I'm not dense." Her face clouds with anger. "I was there with Mom at the end. And I went to the funeral. I heard the words the priest said at the ceremony. I saw…" she shudders, "…the coffins disappear behind the curtain. That's what happens when people are cremated. Did you know that?"

"No." I feel like icy fingers are squeezing my heart.

"Well, it's true!" A tear rolls down her cheek.

I don't know what to say, so I reach over and put my arms around her. This time, she doesn't pull away.

I let her cry into my hair, feeling the warm tears soaking through my top. It's like something inside of her has broken—something that was holding back her emotions like a dam blocks a river. And now, everything needs to come out. That much I understand. I stroke her sleek black hair, as she shudders and sobs against me. I don't know how much time passes, but I know that I'll be here as long as she needs me.

CHAPTER 22

Cake and "Closure"

EVENTUALLY, I PERSUADE VIOLET TO have a piece of cake and a glass of milk. Maybe it's the sugar, or the soft, mellow flavor of the vanilla sponge rippled through with gooey raspberry, but it seems to calm her a little. I listen as everything she's been holding inside her starts to come out.

"The nightmares started a few months back," she says, licking the buttercream off her fork. "I kept seeing myself in the car with them. Though in real life, I wasn't. I'd been unwell that day, so a neighbor came over to look after me. Mom and Dad sang in a choir. They had a concert that night."

"Your mom and dad sound nice."

She wipes away a stray tear. "At the time, I didn't really think too much about it. We were just, you know, normal. Mom worked at an insurance company. Dad taught music at the school. We weren't rich or anything. But family was important to them. I mean, we used to have dinner together every night. Mom cooked. Nothing fancy—just stuff like potatoes and chicken, or shepherd's pie. On the weekends, she'd bake bread, and sometimes she'd cook roast beef and Yorkshire pudding. That was my favorite."

"Wow, Violet, to me they don't sound normal; they sound amazing."

Violet laughs sadly. "Before, I'd have said you were wrong. I got crabby over my homework, or the fact that they wouldn't let me have a phone, or stay up late and watch TV. But now…" She trails off. "I just miss them."

"I'm so sorry," I say. The words sound useless.

"She also made macarons…" She sighs wistfully. "Mom and Dad both loved macarons. Do you know what they are?"

"Um—they're cookies, right?"

"They're little French sandwich cookies, made with almonds and egg whites. You can make them with different colors and flavors in the middle. Though, I've never tried."

"We should make them."

"Maybe sometime." She shrugs noncommittally. "Anyway, then over the last few weeks, the dreams changed. To the ones where I was in my old house but my parents couldn't see me. The counselor thinks that I'm having the dreams because it's been almost two years. Friday's the anniversary of the accident." She shakes her head. "I can't believe it's been that long. I mean, it hurts so much—every day."

She stands and takes her plate to the sink. She seems to be feeling a little better after the cake, but hearing what she's saying, I feel a whole lot worse.

"So what did the counselor tell you to do?" I ask, worried that I might say the wrong thing.

Violet's eyes grow huge and haunted. "She says I have to face up to what happened. Face the fact that there are new people living in my old house now. So, I've decided that I need to go back there."

"Go back? Won't that make it even worse?"

"I don't know. But it's the only way I can think of to get closure."

"Oh?" I puzzle over this. "And what does your aunt say?"

"I haven't told her. Aunt Hilda struggles to talk about what happened—she tries, but it's not easy. I mean, Mom was her sister. She's taken me to put flowers on the grave a few times, but that was hard for both of us. I know she wants me to be happy living with her—and most of the time, I am." She wipes away a stray tear. "I just want the dreams to go away. I want to be able to focus on the good memories, not the bad ones. I don't know if going back there will help, but I've got to try something."

I look away, concentrating on washing up our plates with sudsy warm water. It's taking all my effort to be strong for her. "I want to help, Violet," I say finally. "If there's anything I can do, then you have to tell me. I mean, I had no idea. Maybe I should have..." The guilt floods into my chest but I force it away—this isn't about me. "But really, I didn't know you were going through this. I just thought it was 'boy trouble.'"

"Oh, don't worry, there's that too," she says. "So if you really want to help, then let's make that shortbread." There's a tiny flicker of light back in her eyes. "I may as well find out sooner rather than later if there's any hope of getting Fraser to notice I'm alive."

"He'll notice." I put away the plates and go over to get our aprons.

Or else he's toast, I don't add.

CHAPTER 23

Icing Kisses and Chocolate Hearts

IN THE END, ROSEMARY'S KITCHEN works its magic, or maybe it's the special recipe book, or just the fun we have making the orange and cranberry shortbread with piped-on white chocolate smiley faces (and a few hearts that I insist we do in spite of Violet's reluctance)—but somehow, the hours go by, and it doesn't even feel like time has passed at all. Violet seems back to her normal self, as if the "worry monsters" have stopped sniffing around for the moment.

We chat and laugh and lick the spoons and the bowl, and Violet draws a heart on my cheek with chocolate and I pipe some *X*'s and *O*'s on hers for luck with Fraser. We make a batch of millionaire's shortbread, with a dark chocolate top and a thick layer of sea salt caramel. When I take a bite, I can't believe how delicious it is—the shortbread flaky and the caramel rich and velvety.

"Is this the best we've ever done?" I ask Violet.

"Mm-hmm." She nods, chewing and smiling at the same time.

By the time the shortbread is finished, and we've cleaned up the kitchen, it's after nine. We go through the hole in the wall back to the kitchen in my house and, all of a sudden, it's like a chill wind from the real world has come rushing back.

"Uh-oh," Violet says, checking the screen of her phone. "I have to get home. Aunt Hilda's sent me three texts asking where I am." She quickly types a reply that she's on her way.

"Yeah, sorry. Do you want to take the cookies with you, or do you want me to bring them to school tomorrow?"

"I…don't know." Violet blinks, looking flustered.

"How about we invite him over tomorrow after school? You can surprise him."

"Okay, maybe." She gets her school bag and puts on her cardigan.

"You okay getting home?"

"Yeah. And Scarlett…" Her eyes are once again glassy with tears. "Thanks for everything. You know, especially for listening. I don't know what I'm going to do yet, but I feel a little better."

"Good. I'm here if you need me." I squeeze her hand. "Everything's going to be okay." Outside the warm glow of Rosemary's kitchen, the words sound less certain than I'd like.

When Violet is gone, I take out my phone. In helping Violet with her crisis, I'd forgotten about my own problems—and forgotten to call Producer Poppy.

My sister is in the front room watching TV with Mom—some show about saving a vintage clothing shop somewhere. I pop in and bring them a plate of millionaire's shortbread, leaving them in chocolate heaven while I go up to my room.

When my door is shut, I go to my desk and turn on my new computer. I deliberately avoid checking my emails—I'd been planning on writing a blog post on "cookie flavors for spring" and posting the photos of our scrumptious shortbread. But the words won't come. Not until I know for sure what's lurking in my inbox.

I click on the mail icon. Although I was expecting it, my throat constricts, making it hard to breathe. I open the new message from Dad:

Hi, Scarlett,

I hope you're well. From the sound of things on

your blog, you seem very excited about your mom's wedding. I'm so pleased that everything has worked out for you all, and that all of you will be very happy. Maybe you think I'm just saying it because I should. But the truth is, I do wish you every happiness now and in the future.

Now I'm starting to sound like a greeting card, so I'll stop. But speaking about your future, I want to set the record straight on something else. I know you saw the video your mom posted on her blog at the beginning, saying that I asked her for money. The way she said it—well—I know she was angry and out to gain a following, so maybe things were made to sound a little bit different than they really were. We've discussed it now—ask her if you don't believe me.

Anger bubbles in my veins and I want to slam down the lid of the laptop. How dare he leave Mom, then try to make excuses so that he sounds like the person who was hurt by what happened! I want to write back—tell him to stop bugging me—to get out of my life. But instead, I keep reading:

Before you slam down the lid of the laptop, let me get to the point. I did ask her for money—I wanted to make sure we both put some money away for you and your sister. When her blog got going, I suggested that we each put money into an account. I told her to send me a check, and I'd take care of it. She decided to do the vlog—telling her followers that now that her blog was successful I wanted a share of the money.

I don't blame her. She was angry. I'd hurt everyone. She found a good way to get back at me. In the end, I opened savings accounts for you and your sister, and I put a little in each month. If you ever want or need money for anything, just ask and we'll talk about it.

Love, Dad

The message ends and I do slam down the laptop lid. I'm crying and fuming, and I'm not really sure why. I don't need to know the details of the money stuff—I get the idea. Dad wants me to think that he's in the right, and Mom did something bad to him on her blog.

As if!

I put my head in my hands, and instead of sobbing, I start to laugh. Because the sad truth of it is, I can well imagine that every word Dad wrote is absolutely true.

CHAPTER 24

Twisted Truths

I LIE IN MY BED, staring at the ceiling. I think about Violet and her nightmares. How brave she is to want to confront the bad things head-on. I think about "closure," and the "worry monsters" and wonder if this whole thing with Dad is something that I—and maybe Mom too—need to confront before we can move on. But try as I might, the fear won't go away. Fear of all the changes and the stuff I can't control.

At some point, Kelsie comes upstairs for bed. She sticks her head into my room and asks if she can have another piece of shortbread tomorrow for her lunch. Her chin has a little smear of chocolate on it.

"Sure," I mutter, wishing I was as clueless as my sister, who just seems to bump along with everything that happens, enjoying the presents and the attention from our long-lost dad.

When Kelsie's in her room, I swing out of bed. There's nothing I can do—I have to talk to Mom. I pace my room, trying to gather my courage and think about what I'm going to say. That for all these years I've been hating Dad in part based on the lies Mom's told me. How many more truths did she twist for the purposes of her blog and her followers? I thought that was all behind us now, that we'd worked through how we both felt about what she did—my feeling that she was wrong to write about me in a way that embarrassed me and made me lose confidence; her view was that she did it to earn money for the family—but I see now that I wasn't the only person who was hurt by what she did. Is this newfound "friendship" with Dad her way of apologizing for the lies she told? Or is she trying to turn back the clock and get back with him? How many more people will she end up hurting in the process?

I slip out of my room and start going down the stairs. But halfway down I hear voices coming from the kitchen. Mom—and Em-K. I hesitate, not wanting to get in the middle of a lovers' tiff—or reunion.

"And you've seen him since he's been back?" Em-K's voice sounds unusually high-pitched.

"Oh, once," Mom says breezily. "Maybe twice."

"Are you sure that's a good idea?"

"What's the matter? Are you jealous?" Mom's voice is low, almost like she's purring.

"Should I be?"

Mom laughs. "A little competition is healthy, don't you think?"

"With the wedding coming up so soon, I'm not sure."

"Hey…" Mom stops laughing. "Don't be like that."

I creep down another step.

"He hurt you, remember?" Em-K says. "You told me you were glad he was gone—that you never wanted to see him again."

There's the sound of a cork popping out of a wine bottle, and the glug of liquid pouring into two glasses.

"He's back in town. Living here," Mom says. "I can't just pretend he doesn't exist. He's their father."

"He wasn't too interested in all that when he left, was he? Or in the years afterward. So why now?"

"He's from here—knows people. Besides, he's a grown man. He's got the right to live where he wants."

"I just don't want him spoiling things, that's all."

"He just wants to see the kids—that's it." Mom sounds desperate to convince him. "And I owe him that, surely."

"Do you? Why?"

The breath freezes in my chest.

"Well, I didn't exactly paint him in the best light on the blog, did I? You know, I sort of *embellished* the bad stuff." A glass clunks down on the table. "I told him that if he wants, he can set the record straight with Scarlett. Let her know the truth."

There's a silence for a few seconds. Then Em-K speaks again, his tone lighter, almost playful. "Remind me never to cross you. I wouldn't want your followers sending my career down in flames."

Mom laughs. "Don't worry. I plan on reminding you…as often as I need to."

The conversation stops as the glasses clink together. I've heard more than enough. Way more. I creep back up the stairs to my room and bury my head underneath the pillow.

CHAPTER 25

Facing Up

WHEN I WAKE UP THE next morning, my head hurts. Mom feeling guilty for what she did to Dad. Dad wanting to "set the record straight" and come back into our lives—just before Mom's wedding to Em-K. And Mom twisting the truth to Em-K about how often she's been in touch with Dad.

Then, as I'm walking to school, Producer Poppy phones again. I stop and look down at the lit-up screen, listening to it ring and ring, until finally it stops. I know I need to speak to her, but I just can't face it right now. And then there's Violet... she's left me a message too.

Not feeling so good. Can you ring me?

I scroll through my contacts past the numbers for Alison, Gretchen, Nick...and Violet. The cursor hovers over "Fraser S." I hit the call button.

"Hello," he answers on the fifth ring. There's the sound of traffic in the background. "Scarlett, is that you?"

"Yeah," I say. "I wanted to catch you before school. Can you come over after school, around four thirty? It's…kind of a special thing."

"Well, yeah, I guess so."

"Don't tell anyone, okay? It will be our secret."

"Sure, but…"

I end the call. Let him think what he likes. The only thing I really need is for him to turn up.

But when I get to school, I worry that I've made a mistake. Violet looks a mess. "I didn't sleep," she admits. "I woke up again with nightmares. Mom was in the house, opening all the cupboards, looking for me. I tried to call out, but she couldn't hear me. And then when she turned around, her face…it was…" She shudders. "It was so awful. I tried to go back to sleep, but I couldn't. I didn't even feel like drawing. I just lay there, staring at nothing. I kept thinking about Fraser—how he probably doesn't even know what happened to my parents. When he finds out, he'll think I'm some kind of nutcase or something."

She breaks off, her eyes clouded with tears.

"Hey, look," I say, "you don't have to tell him anything if you don't want to. And we're going to sort it out. I promise."

"I know you're trying to help, but I don't see how…"

"Go home first. I'll see you about five."

Just as well I told Fraser to turn up at four thirty.

In the end, Fraser is late and Violet is early, so they both arrive at the same time. Violet looks a little better—there's a surprised glow about her as she stands next to Fraser on the doorstep and I let them both in. We go through to Rosemary's kitchen, where I've laid out both types of shortbread cookies we made for Fraser on a plate, and have poured milk into three tumblers.

"Cool," Fraser says. "When did you make these?"

"Yesterday. We thought we'd try a Scottish recipe," Violet says. I'm relieved to see that she's not tongue-tied with nerves. In fact, she seems calm and in control—much more than usual.

"It was practice for the wedding menu," I add quickly. "Mom likes shortbread, so I thought we could make them for the tea cookies."

Fraser looks at Violet and takes one of the orange and

cranberry cookies with a chocolate smiley face. "Delicious." He smiles. Her pale face flushes as she quickly hands him another one.

"We thought you'd be the best person to judge them," she says. "Because you're Scottish and all."

The conversation isn't exactly flowing, but the fact that Alison isn't here means that at least Fraser is focusing on Violet.

"Are you up for trying to make macarons today?" I say to Violet. "I found a recipe."

She gives me a long look. "Yeah, I think that would be... good."

"Those are the French cookies, right?" Fraser says. "I've never had them before." He reaches for another shortbread.

Violet takes her sketchbook out of her bag and opens it. The page is covered in little round cookies in all different flavors and colors. "They were my mom's favorite," she says softly. "Maybe we can make them for the school cafeteria. In memory of her."

"In memory?" Though he's about to bite into the cookie, he lowers his hand. I look at her in surprise.

Violet inhales deeply. "Two years ago, something really bad happened..."

Fraser stops eating and listens as she tells him a short

version of what happened. I watch his face—and I know she was right to tell him. It's something that's part of her, and will either scare him away, or prove that he's more than just "nice" on the outside. Still, I can't believe she's being so brave—I certainly wouldn't be.

She talks, and they both eat more cookies. I decide to leave them to it. Neither of them notices as I slip back through the hole in the wall to write a post for the blog.

THE SECRET COOKING CLUB

May 4

This week has been very sweet—literally! We've been making cookies. I remember when I was little and I loved chocolate chip cookies with gooey, moist centers—and even better was eating the dough raw! But nowadays, we're trying to be a little more grown-up. Yesterday, my friend and I made orange and cranberry shortbread, with lots of butter, and chocolate piping on top (yeah—heart-shaped!). We also made a batch of scrumptious millionaire's shortbread—with oozy caramel and chocolate on top. Today, we're going to try making rainbow-colored macarons. In case you aren't sure what those are (I wasn't until yesterday), they're French, and made with ground almonds and egg whites with cream filling in the middle. Or, if you can't eat nuts, some people make them with pumpkin flour! In the end—the outside should be crispy like meringue, and the inside is—whatever flavor you can dream up!

Keep an eye out for the photos!

The Little Cook

xx

In a way, it couldn't have gone better. When I came back to check on them a while later, Violet was in tears, and Fraser had moved around to the other side of the table to sit next to her, and was holding her hand. Mission accomplished!

Seeing me, though, they both looked awkward, and Violet moved her hand away.

"Hi," I say, wishing I hadn't disturbed them. "I was just, um…"

"Fraser said he'd go with us," Violet says. She wipes her eyes with her sleeve and smiles at him.

"Go with us? Where?"

"To the house where I used to live," Violet says. "I've decided that's what I need to do. So I can get…you know… closure."

"Really?" I look at Fraser.

"Um, you're coming too, right?" Violet suddenly looks nervous.

"Well…" If it were a "date," I would definitely have said

no. Some of the awkwardness between me and Nick comes from the fact that we're almost always around other people, never alone just to talk. But this is a lot more than that. Violet needs me. I'm not really sure what visiting her old house is going to do, but I want to be there for her. "Yeah, sure," I say. "Maybe I could see if Nick can come too."

Fraser looks instantly relieved. I'm not sure if that's a good thing or a bad thing.

"Okay," he says. "So when are we going?"

"You two work it out," I say. I grab a piece of millionaire's shortbread off the plate and pop it in my mouth, hoping it will give me courage. "I've got to go and make a phone call."

I go up to my room and stare at my phone. But each time I try to make myself dial Producer Poppy's number, my fingers start to jitter, and I can't bring myself to press the call button. Eventually, I get annoyed with myself and stab in the digits. Violet's been facing up to her problems and taking action. I have to do the same.

The phone rings and I start to feel queasy, then hopeful that it might go to voicemail. But after five rings, it's answered by a breathless, loud female voice. "Hello. Poppy here."

"Um, hi. This is Scarlett. Um…Claire's daughter. You left me a message." My voice rises up like I'm asking a question.

"Scarlett!" she booms. "Great to hear from you. Just give me a sec." The background noise is muffled as she puts her hand over the phone and moves somewhere quieter. "Sorry," she says. "We're in the middle of filming a new dating show for mature women."

"Oh."

"But yes, the wedding show. It will be wonderful having you in to bake the cake. Can you come into the studio for a chat and to look around? Meet the team? Now let's see what I have in the calendar." There's the sound of flipping pages. "Here we go. Let's see, I could do…tomorrow? You could come after school."

"Um…I…" I *need* to stand up to her. Tell her that I'm not doing the show unless the whole Secret Cooking Club is on air too, making the wedding feast.

"It's just that…"

"Just a minute," Producer Poppy says to someone in the background, clearly in a rush.

"So, Scarlett, shall I put you down for say, four o'clock?"

"Um…"

"Great. This is going to be such fun!"

I end the call, my hands shaking. Why couldn't I stick to my guns; tell her that at the end of the day, it's Mom's wedding, and the Secret Cooking Club is going to be involved no matter what issues some TV station may have with that? Why didn't I? Why?

With a sigh, I throw the phone down on the bed. I suppose Violet's right—I do have "stage fright" when it comes to dealing with real people. I don't want them to know the real me, or wonder about me—it's fine doing the blog because that's "The Little Cook," not Scarlett. Maybe it sounds like I'm splitting hairs, but to me, it makes all the difference in the world. Not to mention the fact that I promised my friends I'd make it happen, and it's the Secret Cooking Club that deserves the credit for everything we do, not just one person.

I feel like a storm cloud has gathered over my head as I go back downstairs and through the hole in the wall to rejoin Violet and Fraser. To my relief, they still seem to be hitting it off. Fraser is mixing up the fillings for the macarons— mint, strawberry, double chocolate, lavender—and Violet is adding rainbow gel food coloring to the little pots of almond and egg white mixture. It's like a garden of spring flowers right in the kitchen.

"They look beautiful," I say.

Violet blushes. "Yeah, it's been fun. I'm just about to start piping the macarons. Fraser's going to do the filling. Do you want to help?"

"Okay." I don't want to be a third wheel, but baking is just what I need to get over the stress of *not dealing* with the TV thing.

Violet pipes and Fraser mixes. I put the first batch in the oven, and do some washing up. We chat and laugh, and taste the mixture and the first batch that come out of the oven. It's fun—as usual.

We make four trays of lovely, rainbow macarons. As they're cooling on the racks, we start to clean up the kitchen. Then, after carefully piping in the fillings for one of each flavor, it's the moment we each get to try one. I take a light purple one with lavender crème in the middle. Fraser takes a chocolate one, and Violet a strawberry one. I bite into mine.

"Oh my gosh, this is amazing!" I say. "Even better than the shortbread."

Violet smiles wistfully. "Yeah. I think so too."

"Your mom would be proud," Fraser says.

Violet nods silently. A tear leaks from her eye.

Fraser and I glance at each other. We go back to finish cleaning up to give her some space. Violet eats her second macaron—a light green mint—and puts the rest of the unfilled macarons into a tin. Finally, she turns to me. "How does tomorrow sound?"

"Uh…" I say, feeling like I'm being pulled back to earth. "For what?"

"To visit my old house," Violet says. "It's the, um… anniversary. If that's okay with you, can you check with Nick?"

I think of the wedding, and how Mom's counting on me. I think of the TV producer and about how the whole idea of being on TV by myself is turning my stomach inside out. I think of Dad, and Em-K, the lies Mom told. All of it flashes before my eyes in a rainbow swirl of macarons.

"Sure," I say. "Tomorrow it is."

CHAPTER 26

Going Too Far

AFTER FRASER AND VIOLET LEAVE, I sit in Rosemary's kitchen for a while with Treacle on my lap, stroking his velvety black fur. By the time I go through the wall back to our house, it's after 8:30 p.m. The door to the Mom Cave is closed—which is a relief. Now that I've messed up the meeting with the TV producer, I really don't want a confrontation with Mom.

As I'm about to go to the front room, my sister comes out. "Look, Scarlett!" She points to two big cardboard boxes in the hall. They must have arrived while we were baking because I didn't see them earlier.

"What are those?" I say.

"Dad came by and dropped them off. You just missed him."

"Dad? He came here?"

"Yeah, he dropped Mom off and brought in the presents."

I feel an odd mixture of relief and disappointment that I missed seeing Dad. He's right—it is easier reading what he has to say rather than talking face-to-face. But eventually, I'll have to see him again. One thing's for sure, though—I don't like the fact that he's giving Mom rides and bringing presents.

"Where's Mom now?" I say.

Her face falls. "I don't know. She said she needed to call Em-K and that I should wait till she's done to open the box."

"Okay. I'll go and see her. Practice your Wii singing, okay?"

"But, Scarlett, I've done that already."

"Fine. Watch TV."

I close the door to the front room and go back to the kitchen. The door to the Mom Cave is still shut, and I put my ear next to the keyhole, listening.

"Seriously…" Mom is saying, her voice high and unnatural. "Can't you do this one thing for me?"

Obviously I can't hear the reply, but there's the sound of Mom getting up and pacing the room.

"I know it's a short time. That's why I'm asking."

More silence.

"No—absolutely not. I'm doing the TV show. Or else, well…you can forget the whole thing."

I straighten up and go to the fridge, remembering that I haven't had any dinner. But in truth, I'm not hungry. I know Mom's really stressed right now, but these arguments she's having with Em-K make me really worried. He's usually very calm and rational when they argue, and Mom seems like a great big bully. Especially now.

"Fine. Be like that." I hear Mom's angry words even without listening at the door. Then, there's the sound of something being thrown. Her phone, probably. I've seen it happen before—it's a wonder it still works.

I put some cheese crackers and a wedge of Applewood smoked cheddar on a plate and go back to the front room.

"Please can I open my box?" Kelsie begs.

"What did Mom say?"

"To wait."

"Well, then…"

I sit next to my sister on the sofa and we watch a recording of *Junior Bake-Off*. "I'd love to be on TV," Kelsie says. "Wouldn't you?"

"No," I say between mouthfuls of cheese and crackers. "But I'm sure if you want to when you're older, Mom would love it."

"Love what?"

I turn. Mom's standing at the door. Her hair is messy and she's wearing an old sweatshirt. It's the first time I've seen her looking so rumpled since she started seeing Em-K.

"Nothing, just talking about being on TV," I say. "You okay, Mom?"

"Yes, yes." She waves a hand. "Just the usual. Now, Kels…" She turns to my sister, all smiles. "Let's see what your dad brought you this time, shall we? He's so thoughtful!"

Kelsie attacks the box, ripping at the cardboard while Mom tries to undo the tape. I sit back and watch, dreading the moment when it's my turn to open up the box addressed to me.

"Oh, look, Mom! It's amazing!" Kelsie pulls out a giant brown teddy bear. It has a tag from the toy store around its neck. It's almost as big as my sister, and she hugs it, squealing with delight.

"It's just the one I told him about! Can I call Dad now? I want to say thank you!"

"Sure," Mom says. I stand, ready to take my plate to the kitchen and head upstairs. The whole thing's put a sour taste in my mouth—Mom's fight with Em-K, Kelsie's delight over the present. Rather than a teddy bear, it's more like there's an elephant in the room.

"Aren't you going to open your box, Scarlett?" Mom says from behind me.

I whirl around, anger swimming in my chest. "No, I'm not." I keep my voice low and icy. "I don't need anything from Dad—as in, the man who left us. The man who hurt us, turned his back on us, and sent me five dollars twice a year." I grip the plate tightly in my hand. "The man who waltzes back into our lives just when you're supposed to be marrying Em-K. Unless you drive him away too."

Without meaning to, I've gone too far. Mom's face morphs into something ugly and green.

"How dare you," she spits. She takes a step toward me, and I shrink back. She raises her hand and takes off her ring. She holds it up to her eye, and it glints in the light. Then, she throws it down on the sofa next to me. It bounces off the cushion and on to the floor.

"You think you're so smart, Scarlett, don't you? Always judging me—always complaining. But you don't know anything about being a grown-up—anything at all!"

My sister buries her face in her bear's fur, looking like she might cry. I look past her to where the ring is lying on the floor. Mom makes no move to go and pick it up.

I jump up and run out the door.

"That's it—go on, walk away," she calls after me. "Leave the rest of us here to muddle through. That's what you do, isn't it?"

My whole body is shaking as I stagger up the stairs. Behind me, the door of the front room opens. There's another loud thunk as Mom heaves the box from Dad out into the hall, and then slams the door.

CHAPTER 27

Rainbow Macarons

I STAY IN MY ROOM for the rest of the evening, feeling awful. Why did I pick a fight with Mom—and now, of all times? I know I should go down and apologize—try to talk to her and make things right. But I don't. Half of me expects her to come up, knocking softly on my door the way she often does, asking if we can talk. But she doesn't.

I take out my phone to call Violet, then put it away again. We're supposed to be going to the place she used to live tomorrow after school—it's about an hour away by train. But I'm double-booked with an appointment to see Producer Poppy. I can't let Violet down—she needs me. But if I don't turn up at the meeting, then Mom will be breathing fire.

In the end, I feel so conflicted that I don't cancel either

one. I plug my phone into the charger next to my bed, and turn on my computer. Without even a second thought, I click on the mail icon and read the new one that's come in from Dad:

Hi, Scarlett,

Sorry I missed you earlier. I hope you can make use of the little gift I left for you. I know it's a lot to ask, but I was wondering—would you be able to come over to my apartment one evening so we can talk, just the two of us?

If you did come, maybe I could cook dinner—or we could even do it together? You may not remember, but I used to love to cook. I was pretty bad at it, I admit, but it was something I always enjoyed doing. The smells and the flavors, mixing things together that seem to belong that way—it's a wonderful creative outlet for a guy like me who doesn't have much creativity in the day job. Anyway, it was just a thought. I hope that you're doing well, and that maybe, one day, we can get together.

Love, Dad

There's nothing to do about it—I break down in tears, feeling like my heart is about to tear in two. I'm not quite sure why I'm crying, but it seems like something I should have done a long time ago. I never cried when Dad went away—not really. I suppose in a way, I bottled everything up, just like Violet did when her parents were killed. And now, just like she's facing her demons and her fears, I need to face mine.

I hit reply and type.

Dinner would be nice. Maybe on Saturday?

I press the send key and the little paper airplane symbol zooms off, tearing off a piece of me as it goes.

I don't see Mom the next morning, despite waiting around a little longer at breakfast in the hope she'll come down. I even go up and listen at the door of her bedroom. From inside, there's the sound of typing, just like she used to do in the old days on Friday mornings when her blog post telling the world the gory details of my life would go live at 8 a.m. I want to knock—say sorry, try to patch things up. But just then, Kelsie yells from downstairs that she can't find her PE bag, so to avoid being late for school, I decide to leave it.

On my way out, I go through the hole in the wall and get the tin of macarons. I helped Violet make a sign: IN MEMORY.

We'll fill them at school and leave them in the cafeteria at lunch. There's also plenty of extra for us to eat on the train and, if anyone answers the door at Violet's old house, we'll offer them some too. I tuck the tin under my arm and herd Kelsie out the door. We both have to squeeze past the large box in the hall from Dad that I still haven't opened.

Unsurprisingly, Violet looks worried and stressed all through the day at school. I corner her after lunch in the girls' bathroom. "Are you sure you want to do this?" I say. "You don't have to."

She looks at herself in the mirror, wincing at the dark circles under her eyes and pinching her cheeks to add some color.

"I don't know if I have to or not," she says. "But I'm going to." She turns to me. "Thanks for coming along. I mean, I'm kind of regretting inviting Fraser. Weird date, huh?"

I laugh. "Maybe. But this will be a good test. See if he's worth it?"

"Yeah, I guess. You and Nick okay?"

I think about the question. When I'd texted him about the trip, he'd had something going on—rugby or science club or cross-country—I can't quite remember which. Since baking Dad's cake—which seems like ages ago—I've barely seen Nick other than to say hello in the halls. So I was really glad when he said he'd skip his other thing and come along.

"Yeah." I shrug. "As you say, weird date."

This time, she laughs too.

The four of us meet up after school as planned. We catch a bus to the station and buy our tickets. Violet is putting on a brave face, and luckily Nick chats with Fraser about video games, so there's no lag in the conversation.

As the train pulls up to the platform, I squeeze Violet's hand. She smiles gratefully, and the four of us, plus one tin of macarons, get on the train.

The journey takes an hour. I've already filled Nick in on where we're going and why. I try to join in the conversation between Nick and Fraser, but it's all kind of awkward. Violet mostly stares out of the window. Fraser glances at her from time to time, looking, I think, a bit terrified. I smile encouragingly and give Nick a little elbow to keep talking.

Eventually, we arrive. The station is busy and confusing, and we have to ask three different guards before we find the right bus stop. By the time we finally do, Violet is looking absolutely green. "Seriously, you don't have to do this," I remind her again. "We could go and see a movie or—whatever there is to do around here."

"I'm fine." It's obvious that she's lying.

"You're very brave," I say quietly, so that the others won't hear.

We get off the bus on a main road that could be anywhere. Just off the main road are some streets of small houses, mostly red brick. Violet leads the way, turning down a road called Primrose Gardens. The houses along it are small with neat front gardens, some with small squares of lawn, others paved, and with minivans and cars in the driveways.

She stops in front of a small house with rough white plaster on the upper floor. There's a small porch with No. 14 on it. The front door is framed by two pots of red geraniums. Around the side of the house, there's a pink tricycle parked next to the recycling bins. There's a package left on the mat, and no car in the driveway. Whoever's living there must be out.

"This is it," Violet says. Her face is pinched and ghostly white.

Now that we're here, I've no idea what we need to do to get her the closure she needs. I reach out and grip Nick's hand. He gives mine a squeeze, but I can tell he doesn't have a clue either.

"Should we ring the doorbell and see if anyone's home?" Fraser says.

Violet shakes her head. Her grip on the tin of macarons loosens a little. "No one's home," she says. "But it doesn't matter. I see that now."

She plops down on the curb outside the house. Silently, she opens the tin.

I'm not sure what to do, so I sit next to her.

"What flavor would you like?" she says.

"I don't know…um…mint."

"Good choice."

She hands me a green macaron. Nick and Fraser take the hint and sit too—Nick next to me, and Fraser next to Violet. She doles out macarons to them—chocolate for Nick and lavender for Fraser.

"The house looks totally different," she says, taking a pink macaron from the basket. "It used to be painted gray. And did you see the tricycle? They must have a kid."

"Yeah." I'm totally baffled by the sudden change in her attitude and don't know what to say.

"I remember…" she continues, "…how my mom taught me to ride a bike without training wheels. I was so mad because I thought I couldn't learn. But I didn't even know when she let go." She opens the macaron and licks at the rose-pink filling. "And when we came back inside, Dad made me a big mug of hot chocolate with whipped cream and candy sprinkles." She smiles. "I think that's why I've got such a sweet tooth now."

"What color was your bike?" Fraser asks. He alone seems unfazed.

"Pink glitter, of course!" Violet giggles. "With silver streamers on the handlebars."

"Of course!" Fraser laughs.

She passes out more macarons—each one beautiful and tasting so different. I try a strawberry one. The outside is crunchy and the filling is slightly bittersweet. It seems right somehow.

"And did your mom cook?" Nick asks. "Is that where you get your talent from?"

"Well, I don't know about talent." Violet's pale cheeks flush. "But yes, she did. She used to bake bread—on Saturdays. I remember that. It was the best bread ever. Really soft on the inside, with a crisp crust. It took her forever to make it. But she did." She bites into another macaron, smiling at the memory.

"Which one was your room?" I finally find my voice.

"It was at the back. The walls were yellow, and I had a Disney Princess bed. It was covered with stuffed toys. Mom used to say that there was no room for—"

She stops speaking as a blue car pulls into the drive. A blond-haired woman a little younger than Mom gets out. She doesn't seem to notice us, but goes around to the back doors of the car to unstrap two small children—a girl with her ginger hair in pigtails, and a boy wearing a football shirt. The mom opens the trunk and takes out two overflowing bags full of groceries. A box of cereal falls out on to the driveway. Nick runs up and hands it to her.

"Thanks," she says, eyeing him suspiciously. She then notices the rest of us. "Uh, can I help you?" she says.

"No, thanks." Violet stands. "We were just leaving." She closes the tin and starts to walk away.

"Hey, wait a minute," Fraser calls after her. He turns to the woman. "She used to live here," he says. "She came by to see her old house."

"Oh, really?" The woman sets down her shopping bags. Nick immediately picks them up and carries them up to the door. "It's a nice house," the woman says. "We just moved here—last year. The schools are good. And my mom lives around the corner."

"Mom, I'm hungry!" the little boy shouts.

"Can we have pizza?" the girl says.

"Sorry, but…" The woman shakes her head, clearly eager to get inside. "I mean, do you want to come in or something?"

Violet turns back to the woman. "No, that's okay. Really.

I've seen what I need to see." A spark seems to have returned to her eyes. "And I think someone's hungry!"

She winks at the two small children.

"Were you eating cookies?" the boy asks her.

"Oh…maybe." Violet grins.

"Mom, can we have a cookie after dinner?"

"I don't know…we'll see." The woman unlocks the door. The two children run inside. "Are you sure you don't want to come in?"

"I'm sure." Violet grabs my hand and squeezes it. I'm not quite sure what has—or hasn't—happened, but I know she means it.

"Okay." The woman doesn't quite manage to hide her relief. She's obviously got her hands full without uninvited visitors. She lifts the groceries inside the door. "Well, goodbye then." She smiles at Violet and closes the door.

"Are you sure you don't want to go inside, Violet?" Fraser looks a little distressed. "I mean, she said you could—at least for a few minutes. To see your room or whatever."

"Really, it's okay." She rests her hand lightly on his arm. "I've got what I came for. I can't really explain it, but I feel a lot better. I mean, there's a new family in the house now. That's a good thing, I think. Now they can have happy memories there too."

"Okay…" Fraser hesitates.

"But there is one thing. Scarlett, do you think you can spare this tin?"

I smile, knowing exactly what she wants to do.

"I think I can."

I take the tin from her hand, and go up to the front door. I leave it on the mat and ring the doorbell. Then the four of us run off down the road and out of sight.

CHAPTER 28

Turning a Corner

AS WE STAND AT THE bus stop waiting for the bus, none of us really speaks. Nick and Fraser look a little shell-shocked, but I sense that for Violet, a kind of peace has set in.

"Is there anything else you want to do?" I say softly, so only she can hear.

"Yeah." She grins. "I want to go home."

I nod, smiling too. I guess that by coming here to her old house, she's turned a corner. Some of her memories are painful, but there are happy ones too. Maybe today has helped her see that—that for her, closure is about seeing the whole picture, not just the bad stuff. And maybe that's what I need to do too—with Dad, and Mom. So many times I've wished I had a recipe to deal with all the changes; all the things I can't control. But I know that doesn't exist. One thing I can do is face up to things the way Violet's done. Knowing that, though, doesn't make it a lot easier to do in reality.

We've already got our return tickets, so when we reach the station, the four of us go through the barrier to wait on the platform. I look up at the board—the train's delayed by forty-five minutes due to a signal failure.

"Bad luck," Fraser says, pacing a few steps down the platform.

"Yeah," I say.

Violet looks up from the screen of her phone. "Um, Scarlett?" she says. "You told your mom where you were going, right?"

"Not exactly," I say. My stomach knots. Coming here today might have helped Violet ditch her bag of worries—but now I feel like it's me who's carrying the extra weight.

Nick, who also has his phone out, takes it away from his ear. "She seems a little upset," he answers for Violet. "I got a text and a couple of voicemails. Did you forget your phone?"

"Yeah," I sigh. "I guess I did."

Violet raises her eyebrows. She knows good and well that I'm never without my phone and must have "forgotten" it on purpose. Which isn't exactly true. After last night—the fight with Mom, the thrown ring, the message from Producer

Poppy, and the email to Dad—I plugged it in next to my bed to charge. And this morning, I "managed" to leave it behind. One meeting with Producer Poppy—sorted.

"You'd better listen to her messages." Violet holds out her phone. I take it, and press the play button.

In the first message, Mom just sounds annoyed:

Violet—have you seen Scarlett? She's supposed to be at a meeting at the TV station. Right now.

In the second, the annoyance is mixed with concern:

Violet—Scarlett's phone is in her room. I don't know where she is. I'll try Nick too. Call me if you've seen her.

And in the third, it's genuine concern:

Violet? Are you there? Why are none of you answering? I'm worried. We had a bit of a fight last night. If I don't hear from her by six, I'm calling the police.

I check my watch. Five minutes to six. I dial her number. It immediately goes to voicemail.

"Hi, Mom," I say. "I'm fine. You don't need to call the police. Sorry I missed the meeting—I umm…forgot."

My three friends are looking at me. I end the call.

"Sounds like you're in trouble," Nick says, his grin mischievous.

"I was supposed to meet Producer Poppy." I take a

breath. "I didn't want to say anything, but she didn't like the idea of the whole club being on TV. Something about it being too much work for the TV station. I need to convince her. But I've…well…kind of been avoiding the whole thing."

Nick brushes my hand lightly. I feel a spark jump between us. "Look, Scarlett. This TV thing isn't worth getting stressed about. It would have been fun, but it's really no big deal."

"But Gretchen…"

"…will get over it," Violet finishes.

Fraser nods. "We can still do the menu. For something else. My sister is getting married next year. Maybe we can surprise her with a spread from the Secret Cooking Club."

"Maybe." Violet smiles at him, her eyes melty.

"Thanks," I say. "But I'm not giving up that easily. I will call her and get this sorted out."

A notice flashes up on the board—the train is delayed by another thirty minutes.

"We'd better get comfortable," Fraser says. He points to the waiting room, and we all troop inside to sit down. When, at six o'clock, Mom still hasn't called back, I borrow Nick's phone and try calling her again. Once again, I get her voicemail.

I decide to try Em-K. The phone rings several times, and just as I'm waiting for the click of voicemail, he answers.

"Emory Kruffs," he answers in his deep politician voice. "How can I help you?"

"Hi, Em-K, it's me."

"Scarlett! Where are you? Your mom's frantic."

"Sorry!" I say. "I left my phone at home. I'm…uh…we're at the train station." I tell him where.

"Your mom's out driving around looking for you. She's called all your friends. Your dad too. How could you be so inconsiderate? She…" he hesitates, "…she thought you'd run away."

"Run away? No!"

"She said you and she had a fight."

"That was last night!" I protest. "Sorry, Em-K. Really I am. But I promised Violet I'd go with her to…" I glance over at my friend, "…never mind. Anyway, we're at the station now but the train is delayed." I look up at the board. It's now showing a fifty-three-minute delay. But just then, the announcer comes over the loudspeaker. *I am sorry to announce that the 5:55 p.m. train is canceled.*

"Um, actually, it's canceled," I say.

He gives a long sigh. "I guess I'll have to come and get you then."

"Would you? That'd be great."

"I should be there in forty-five minutes, depending on traffic. Get yourself some dinner—I'll pay for it. Because when you get home, I don't think anyone's going to feel like cooking."

"Sure," I say warily. "Thanks."

I end the call, knowing that I'm seriously in the doghouse. But part of me feels good as well. That I've got someone like Em-K to look out for me.

"Let's go and get some dinner," I say. "Em-K's paying. He's coming to get us."

"Good," Nick says. "I'm starving."

CHAPTER 29

Another Fight

I'M EXPECTING TO BE IN deep trouble when I get home. It's almost eight thirty by the time Em-K has dropped off my friends and we pull up outside our house. In the car, we told him all about where we went, and why. He seemed more proud of us than angry (though he did give me a talking-to for worrying Mom, which is fair enough, I guess).

When the two of us come into the house, Mom is standing at the door like she's been waiting for us there the whole time (though I can hear the sound of the TV coming from the front room). "Scarlett," she says, giving me a hug. "I was so worried."

"Sorry, Mom," I say. "I forgot my phone."

Ignoring me, she looks at Em-K. "You sure took your time."

A wounded look crosses his face. "I had to drop off the other kids," he says.

Mom holds up her hand. "I'm not even going to ask." She turns back to me. "Your dad and I were frantic with worry."

"Dad?" The word comes out of my mouth before I can stop it. I look again at Em-K. His lips form a thin line.

"Well, of course," she says, frowning. The good feeling she's had at seeing me back is obviously starting to wear off. "Your dad loves you. He wanted to call the police. I told him you're sensible and wouldn't do anything foolish."

"That's right, Mom, I wouldn't." I turn to Em-K. "I'm sorry you had to spend your whole evening getting us. Can I put the kettle on for you?"

He looks questioningly at Mom. "Claire?"

"Go on, the pair of you." She shakes her head, clearly exasperated. "I'm going up to bed. This has all just been one more thing I don't need."

Em-K turns to me. "Thanks for the offer, but I think I'd better be going." There's hurt and anger in his voice.

With a disinterested shrug, Mom stalks back into the front room without saying goodbye. Em-K and I stand there without moving as she calls Dad. She tells him that I'm home, and I'm expecting her to end the call. But she doesn't.

"Bye, Scarlett." Em-K turns and opens the front door. "Sleep well."

My throat wells up. "Thanks, Em-K," I say. "See you soon."

He doesn't answer or look at me as he goes out of the door.

I stand there in the hall, feeling like I'm on the edge of a tall building, looking over the edge. In the other room, Mom is still on the phone with Dad. They talk for what seems like forever, and whatever he says makes her laugh. I can't listen anymore. I go into the kitchen and boil the kettle to make some instant hot chocolate. No matter how "worried" Mom and Dad were about me, it's Em-K who came to get us, and he's the one who Mom will barely even talk to. It strikes me that maybe Mom is making history repeat itself. No wonder Dad left if he was being treated like that.

Eventually, Mom comes into the kitchen. Now that there's no one else around, her worry has turned to irritation. "Never do that again, Scarlett," she says icily.

"I'm sorry, Mom." I grip the hot cup tightly in my hand. The last thing I want is another fight.

"I spoke with Poppy. She wants you in the studio on Sunday to do the filming. And I don't want to hear that you're hanging out with your friends, or visiting old people's homes, or whatever. I'll drive you there myself."

"Sunday! But that's only two days—"

Ignoring me, Mom leaves the kitchen, slamming the door. I push my cup away—there are some things that even hot chocolate can't fix.

· CHAPTER 30 ·

Wedding Tiers

I WAKE UP EARLY THE next morning—Saturday—with my pulse racing. I'm supposed to go on TV to make the wedding cake—tomorrow! I haven't even done a trial run on the whole cake yet, and I also haven't spoken to Producer Poppy to plead with her that my friends be allowed to join me.

Last night, Mom was so angry. I feel like we're back to the old days when we couldn't talk to each other and don't understand each other. The only way I know to make things right is to do the TV show. I can't possibly back out now.

I go downstairs and make a piece of toast, but my mouth is so dry that it tastes like cardboard. I wash it down with a glass of orange juice and try to pull myself together. I'll do a practice bake of the cake today. Mom is supposed to be going shopping, but luckily she didn't ask me to go. And as for the rest—we'll just have to see.

When I've finished washing up my dishes, I go through the hole in the wall to Rosemary's kitchen. As I push aside the curtain of plastic trash bags, I wonder if things will work out and eventually someone will put up a door? Or will the wall be bricked up and plastered over?

As usual, it's warm and quiet, except for the hum of the fridge. *I can do this.* I've baked so many cakes in this kitchen, experimented with so many recipes, there's no reason for me to feel nervous and on edge. But I do.

Treacle is in his basket, licking his paws. "I can do this," I say aloud. He raises his head and flicks his tail. I text Violet. She might want to talk after our trip yesterday. Closure or no, it can't be easy coming to grips with the things that have haunted her for so long. And, from a purely selfish perspective, I could use her decorating skills. I've decided to make little fondant icing figures of Mom and Em-K for the top of the cake. The rest of the decorations will be flowers made of sugar paste and some real edible flowers sprinkled with sugar and glitter. When I described it to Violet before, she made a sketch in her little drawing notebook. It was so beautiful—I could really use the inspiration now.

I take our special recipe book off the shelf of cookbooks and open the red-and-green marbled cover, flipping through to the recipes for cakes. Though Violet and I had joked about a six-tier cake, for today, at least, I'm going to practice one of the flavors we've decided on: the lemon and lavender sponge sandwich cake with fresh strawberries and cream in the center. I'd been looking forward to trying out the recipe—and tasting the cake! But this morning, I can't seem to shift the unsettled feeling in my stomach. Mom, Em-K…Dad…I need to push all the doubts out of my mind.

I cream together butter and sugar with a wooden spoon, adding the eggs one at a time and beating them into the mixture. I've started to measure out the flour when I hear Mom's voice coming through the hole in the wall. She sounds stressed and harried. I assume she's trying to get Kelsie to hurry up and get ready, but then I hear a man's voice—Em-K. I stop what I'm doing.

"I don't know what's up with you, Claire," he's saying. *"But whatever it is, it's got to stop. We're supposed to be getting married—and it's like I hardly know you."*

I add a teaspoon of baking powder to the flour and stir it in.

"This isn't a good time, Emory. We were just on our way out."

I sift the flour into the egg mixture, folding carefully and adding the lavender and lemon zest. I check the recipe again. Flour, sugar, butter, eggs, baking powder...

"I know you're stressed, and that the wedding is taking up all your time. But we didn't have to do it so fast. I never wanted a big wedding, as you know..."

I've missed something—what is it? Baking powder? I add a teaspoon and stir it in. On the table in front of me, my phone vibrates. I stop mixing and check the screen. It's Violet, texting back, asking if she should come over later. Yes please! I reply.

Mom's yelling now. *"No, of course you didn't want it, Emory! You want a wife who cooks your dinner and irons your shirts, and who looks pretty standing behind you at political events!"*

"You know that isn't true! If I wanted that, I would never have asked you to marry me."

My hands are trembling as I finish stirring and pour the mixture into two round baking pans.

"Great—so you're saying I'm not good enough for you?"

"No—that's not what I'm saying. But this is madness. Let's forget this whole big wedding," Em-K says. *"Let's elope—we'll go to the registry office with the girls and a few friends. Then we can have a nice lunch out, and we won't have all the stress."*

"A nice lunch out!" Mom's voice is high-pitched and

furious. Treacle jerks awake, the fur on his back raised. He runs out of the back door through his cat flap. I can hardly blame him. I put the cakes in the oven, and pace back and forth in front of the oven, trying not to listen.

"Is that all I mean to you?" Mom says. *"Because if that's the case, why are we even doing this?"*

I need to find something to distract me, so I sit at the table and open the pack of fondant icing. It was really lucky that I was able to find a pack of twelve different colors, including light pink, black, brown, and white. I roll the fondant in my palms and mold two heads, and four round balls for hands out of the light pink color.

"Well, it's obvious that there's nothing that I can say to reassure you," Em-K replies. *"So why don't you go and ask him? He seems to be the only one you'll talk to right now!"*

I put on two green eyes and red pouty lips for Mom, and blue eyes for Em-K. Then I make the hair, rolling the fondant out into long, thin snakes in my hand. Black hair for Em-K, long brown hair with a few yellow highlights for Mom.

Mom gives that awful laugh. *"I'm not going to apologize for that. He was my husband—the father of my kids."*

"No, you won't be apologizing, will you? Because nothing is ever your fault, Claire, is it?"

I do Mom's dress, which is pretty easy to make—all white and puffy. I'll cover it with glitter or something. When I've finished, I prop the little figures up against the cookbook stand. To be honest, they look pretty awful. Hopefully Violet or one of the others can make something better. But for now, they'll do.

Mom and Em-K keep arguing, and I keep trying not to listen. The smell of the cakes baking—normally one of my favorite scents in the whole world—is making me feel nauseous.

I check the clock. It's been twenty minutes, so I decide to open the oven.

Steam pours out when I open the oven door. I close my eyes and try to enjoy the warm scent of lavender and lemon. But when I open my eyes, I realize the middle of the cakes are cone-shaped and swollen like a volcano ready to erupt.

The dread in my stomach rises as I reach inside the oven and pull out the shelf. The breath goes out of me like a punctured balloon. The cakes…my beautiful cakes…

The edges are just browned on top—perfectly baked from the look of things. But the middles now look like two meteors have crashed down from the sky and landed right in the center. I've never had a cake collapse before. And if there's a first time for everything, it couldn't possibly have come at a worse moment.

"We need to go. And so do you," Mom says.

Hot, salty tears flood my eyes. It's not a disaster. I'll just start over—it will only take twenty minutes to whip up the mixture, and this time, I'll make sure not to get distracted; use the right amount of baking powder. The new cakes won't over-rise like a doughy volcano, collapsing in on themselves at the last second. I'll just pretend that none of this ever happened...

"Fine, I'll go. Goodbye."

I dump the collapsed cakes in the trash. I don't even feel like trying a tiny bite to see if they tasted good. I go back over to the mixing bowl and the ingredients set out on the table. Instead of getting back to work, I sit down and put my head in my hands.

In the other room, the front door slams. The little figure of the bride stares up at me. I've got extra-light pink fondant, so I roll another head. For the hair, I combine yellow and brown—darkish blond like mine. I consider making another dark suit, but then think, why bother? If I need to, I can just change the head at the last minute. Because right now, the only thing I can do is to try to be prepared...

For whichever one of them is going to be my "new dad."

THE SECRET COOKING CLUB

May 6

I want to set the record straight about something. When I read over the posts I've written in the last few months, it sounds like everything is perfect, and that everything I bake is delicious and amazing. But you know what—that's not true. I love to cook, and I do find it relaxing, fun, and creative. But I've got problems just like everyone else, and cake can't solve everything.

Speaking of cake...I did a practice of Mom's wedding cake earlier today. It was, I'm sorry to say, a complete disaster. I used too much baking powder and the whole top exploded in the oven and then collapsed. I guess I'm lucky that it wasn't the real thing—I'll have another chance to get it right.

But the point is, sometimes things like that happen. All we can do, I guess, is try again and not give up.

I should have taken a photo of the exploded cake to show you, but I was too upset and threw it in the trash. Sorry...

The Little Cook

xx

· CHAPTER 31 ·

The Big Collapse

THE HOUSE FEELS AS IF someone's died—it's very quiet and still. Mom and Kelsie go out to the store. When Violet arrives, I tell her everything that happened in the short time since we saw each other last—the collapsed cake, the filming tomorrow— and about the arguments between Mom and Em-K.

"I'm not sure if she threw him out, or if he stormed out—or a little of both," I say, my voice high and strained. "Either way, he's gone."

"So, do you still have to do the TV show?" Violet says, her brow furrowed in concern. "I mean, is the wedding still on?"

"I don't know!" I say. My head feels like it's going to explode. "The whole thing is just so upsetting. I mean, Mom was so happy when Em-K proposed. And now it's gone pear-shaped. All I know is that I've committed to go to the TV studio tomorrow, and if I don't do that, then I may as well pack my bags."

"Hey," Violet says. She takes my hand and squeezes it. "It's going to be okay."

Tears begin to prickle in my eyes. "But what if it isn't?" I blurt out. "I mean, I probably shouldn't care—it's not like I'm the one getting married. It's just, I like Em-K, and he's good for Mom—for us. Things are…I don't know…normal when he's around. Less chaotic. And besides, what if…" I trail off.

"What if what?"

I stare at her for a long time without speaking. She's been through so much more than I ever have, and she's so brave. I wish some of that could rub off on me. But if it's ever going to, then I have to start facing things head-on. Like she did.

"What if Mom is still in love with Dad?" I say. "What if Dad's come back into our lives to split up Mom and Em-K? What if Dad comes back, and then leaves us again? What will Mom be like if Dad comes back?"

Violet shakes her head. "I can't answer that," she says. "But whatever they're doing, it isn't fair. I mean, we have enough to worry about with school and boys and stuff, without worrying about grown-ups and their problems, don't we?"

"You're so brave, Violet," I say. "And I was so proud of you yesterday. I'm not half as strong as you are."

She blinks away a tear glittering like a crystal at the corner of her eye. "It was hard," she says. "But I'm glad I did it. Going there helped remind me of the good times that we had, but it also showed me that there's no going back. All I can do now is move on."

"You'll be fine," I say. "And Fraser—if he's worth anything, he'll totally see what a great person you are."

She brightens instantly. "Guess what?" she says. "He texted me this morning. He's asked me to the spring food fair with him and his mom. It's next weekend."

"That's great!" I grin. "I'm so happy for you. It will be completely fab! I just know it."

"Thanks." She beams. "He said that he was proud of me too."

"I'm sure. And take some photos of what you see at the food fair. Who knows, maybe you'll get some last-minute ideas for the wedding…" I hesitate. "That is, if there is a wedding."

She straightens up. "You need to talk to them, Scarlett," she says. "It's the only way. There's no sense worrying about it until you know what everyone's thinking."

"You're right." I sigh. "But Mom's out, and Em-K…well,

I don't think I should call him till I've talked to Mom. I don't want to put my foot in it. But maybe..." I take a breath as my chest tightens with nerves, "...I could talk to Dad. He asked me if I wanted to come for dinner at his apartment."

"That's a good place to start," Violet says. "You can ask him what he's doing, waltzing in like that and making a mess of everything."

"Yeah," I say, feeling stronger now. "That's exactly what I'm going to do. I'll text him right now." I take out my phone. "The sooner it's over with, the better."

I text Dad asking if we're on for tonight. He replies almost immediately. If it's okay with your mother, it's great for me! Unless I hear otherwise, I'll come get you about 6. Dad

As soon as the plans are made, I instantly regret it.

"Come on, Scarlett," Violet says. "Chin up. Why don't we go and make something for you to bring over for dessert? A peace offering."

"Okay." I sigh. "But you pick something."

"Fine. Let's go."

CHAPTER 32

Eton Mess

AT TEN MINUTES TO SIX, I look out of the window of the front room, clutching for dear life the plastic container with the Eton mess—a yummy mix of berries, meringue, and whipped cream mixed up in a jar—Violet and I made earlier. While it was fun making it, any brave feeling I had then is long gone. The only saving grace was that Mom was so preoccupied with her own problems when she got home from shopping that it barely even registered when I said I wanted to go over to Dad's tonight. "Fine," she'd said. She'd disappeared into the Mom Cave, and that was that.

Not the case, though, for my sister. She opened the box Dad left for me, which turned out to be a fake, leopard-fur-covered beanbag chair. I don't really want to like it, but I do—and so does my sister. The beanbag is so big, fluffy, and soft that I can barely see my sister sitting in it, but I hear her loud and clear as she slams her Wii controller down on to the floor. "Please, Scarlett," she begs in a whiny voice, "I really want to come too."

"No," I say firmly. "Dad's taking you to the shop to get a scooter tomorrow. Tonight is just me and him."

"It's not fair!" my sister pouts. She obviously thinks I'm seeing Dad because I *want* to hang out with him, rather than to confront him.

A car pulls up to the house.

Kelsie bolts outside before I can stop her.

"Kelsie!" I yell.

She runs up to the car and when Dad gets out, she gives him a big hug. He lifts her up and gives her a kiss, then sets her back down. "Please, Daddy, can I come too?" she asks, giving him her best droopy puppy-dog eyes. Dad looks up and sees me standing on the path, stony-faced.

"No, Kels," he says, ruffling her hair. "I'll see you tomor-row. Tonight, I want to spend some time with your sister."

"You're so mean!" Kelsie yells, stamping her foot like she's some kind of toddler.

"Kelsie, come here!"

I turn. Mom's standing at the door. I scan her face, holding my breath as I wait to see how she's going to act around Dad.

"I hate you!" Kelsie runs up the path to the house and storms inside past Mom.

"See you later, Claire," Dad says. "I'll drop her back about nine, if that's okay."

"Fine."

I'm relieved Mom doesn't stick around to chat. Relieved, that is, until she's gone—back into the house—and I'm left standing next to the car. Alone with Dad.

"Hi," I say, my voice hoarse.

"It's good to see you, Scarlett." His tone is matter-of-fact, not all gushy. That, at least, I appreciate.

"Yeah."

He holds the door open for me to get in the car. As we drive off, I can see Kelsie's face pressed to the window in the front room. More than anything, I wish I were there and she were here.

It's only about a ten-minute drive from our house to Dad's new apartment. It feels odd to think that he's so close by, and yet he might as well be a universe away. We chat a little as he drives. He asks me about school and what subjects I like. I tell him I like history and science, and I don't like speech and drama.

"I used to like history and science too," he says. "And luckily, I never had to do any of that drama stuff." He beams at me. I briefly smile back.

I ask him how work is. He answers that his job is less stressful than his previous one, and he likes the project with the TV station. I feel like we're doing a kind of dance—circling around the real issues, neither of us wanting to move beyond small talk. But somehow, I get the sense that he's as nervous as I am.

Eventually he pulls up on a little street near where Alison lives. The houses are made of brick, with tiny front gardens, some that have been paved over for car parking spaces. He pulls up into a space on the street. "Here we are," he says. "Home, sweet home."

He leads the way though a little gate. His front garden is filled with stones, and in the center there's a tree that's sprouting green leaves. The top part of the house is painted white. It looks neat and tidy—much more so than our house. He unlocks the front door, and I follow him inside to a hallway with black and white tiles on the floor. "There's a studio apartment down here," he says, pointing to a door off the hall. "I've got the top two floors."

I don't say anything as I climb the stairs behind him. At the top of the stairs is a little landing. He unlocks the door to the apartment.

The apartment is bigger than it looks from the outside. The whole first floor is open plan with a big window in the front overlooking the street. At the back is a good-sized kitchen and a little dining area. The kitchen overlooks a garden at the back. I can see the other gardens of the nearby houses and, a little way down, a church steeple.

"It's nice," I say, meaning it. The room is painted a creamy-white color, and Dad has only a few pieces of furniture, but it seems like enough. I recognize an old rug from Peru hanging on the wall—it used to be in our old house. There's also some framed school portraits of Kelsie and me up on the wall. There are no pictures of Mom or of us as a family.

"I like it," he says. "It suits me. I have everything I need, and there's two bedrooms upstairs. One is my study. I can do quite a lot of work at home. Plus…" he winks, "…there's a fantastic little Indian takeout restaurant around the corner."

"Sounds good." I feel something building inside me like a wave. I like this apartment. I could see myself coming here sometimes. Doing my homework, having some peace and quiet. Someplace where there isn't a lot of stuff everywhere, and where the TV isn't on all the time, and where I don't have to worry about what kind of mood Mom's in, or about my sister annoying me...

But that future—one where Dad's a part of my life—isn't going to happen. It can't happen. Not until I find out why I'm here, and why now.

"Would you like a drink?" Dad asks. "I've got juice, and tea, and Diet Coke. Or water."

"No." I walk over to him. "I don't want anything. Not until we talk."

He nods gravely. "I understand." He sits at the table. I sit opposite him. I feel like I'm a police officer and he's a criminal, or maybe it's the other way around.

"Ever since you've come back, things have gone pear-shaped," I say. "Mom was happy—she was going to marry Em-K. She and I were getting along. Kelsie was getting used to the idea of a new stepdad—and she loved the idea of being a bridesmaid. But now..." I take a breath. "I don't know. They're fighting all the time, and she's being really horrible to him."

"Isn't that just wedding nerves?"

"I want to know if you're trying to stir things up. Make her not marry Em-K. I want to know if you're trying to come back in our lives." I break off, feeling tears well up in my eyes. I've said way too much. Mom will probably be furious.

Dad is silent for a long moment. He stares at his hands. "Scarlett, I promise you, I am not trying to 'stir things up.' That's not why I moved back here. I love you and your sister, and your mother too—she was my wife and is the mother of my two girls." He smiles. I don't smile back.

"I realized that I'd made a mistake long before your mom told me she was remarrying."

I shift in my chair, uncomfortable.

He holds up a hand. "Not a mistake in letting your mom get on with her life. Things were never going to work out between us. I'm sorry to say that, but it's the truth."

I nod mutely.

"The mistake was leaving like I did. Without accounting for the impact it would have on you, and then moving so far away." He sighs. "I guess I thought that would make the break easier. And in some ways, maybe it did. But there hasn't been a day gone by when I didn't wonder about you and your sister, and how you were getting along…and miss you." His voice catches.

"So, to answer your question, Scarlett, I do want to be

back in your life. Though I have no right to think that you'll want me or have me." He smiles sadly. "I'd love to be able to see you from time to time. Maybe even cook with you. Believe it or not, I used to love to cook."

"You mentioned that in your email."

"Yes." He smiles. "Not that I was very good at it, mind you. But that's not what matters. It was the process I liked. Adding a little of this, a little of that—and getting something completely different at the end, if that makes sense."

It makes perfect sense. "You made spaghetti Bolognese once," I say. "I remember. It was good."

"That's what I was going to make tonight. It's my 'specialty dish.'" He holds up his hand and whispers, "More like, the only thing I can guarantee will be edible."

"Sure."

"Or we could order out—or go out. Whatever you want. I'm just happy that you're here."

"So, you don't want to marry Mom again?" I say. Right now, I'm not sure how whatever he answers will make me feel.

He shakes his head. "There's a Buddhist saying that 'you can't step twice into the same river.' Your mom and I had our chance. It didn't work out. I'm happy that she's happy with Emory."

"Well…I thought she was. But I know the two of you have been talking a lot—going for coffee. It seemed weird—and I know it bothers Em-K."

Dad sighs. "That was probably a bad idea. But she said she didn't have many friends and wanted someone to talk to other than the groom-to-be. And she also wanted to clear the air about what happened between us. To try and make sure that history doesn't repeat itself." He smiles. "Not that I think it will. Em-K seems a much more sensible guy than I am."

"I guess it's nice if you can be friends—as long as that's all you are."

"Scarlett…" He looks me straight in the eye. "That's all we are—I promise."

"Okay." I risk a smile. "Thanks…Dad."

CHAPTER 33

A New Member

DAD CHOPS VEGETABLES AND I cook the meat. When that's done, we put everything into a pot, add salt, pepper, tomatoes, oregano, and plenty of garlic, and I stir the Bolognese sauce over low heat. We chat a little about cooking—what my favorite things are to cook—what his are—and about the Secret Cooking Club.

"Your friends sound very special," he says. He puts a pan of water on the stove to boil.

"They are. And we were all set to cook the wedding food too." I tell him all about the menu we wanted to do, and how we wanted to get as many kids helping us as we could. I tell him about Annabel Greene and how keen she was to help. Then I tell him about Producer Poppy and how what we wanted to do "just won't work."

"Why not?" Dad says, frowning.

"I don't know. She says it will be too complicated and they aren't 'equipped' for that."

"But they have a whole TV studio that's a kitchen. I've seen it."

"I'm supposed to be going there tomorrow," I say, suddenly breathless. "But to be honest, I'm petrified." I tell him about my stage fright and about how ever since Mom put me in the spotlight with her blog, I've hated the idea of people knowing stuff about me.

"That's understandable." He sounds like he's thinking over what I've been saying. One thing I never realized before—Dad's a pretty good listener.

"You think so?"

"I think you should stick to your guns. You'll do the show with your friends, but not on your own. If that's what you want."

"That's what I want."

"Do you think you could get them to come along with you tomorrow? It's pretty short notice."

"I don't know. I could try. We often meet on Sundays anyway."

"If you want to make a few calls, I can finish up the food."

"But what about the producer?"

He gives a cryptic smile. "I've been doing some work at the TV station—as you know. I've run into Poppy before. I could make a call or two after dinner, if you like."

He winks at me, and somehow, I get the idea that he knows her better than he's letting on. "Really?" I say. "Do you think that will work?"

"I can't promise anything, but it's worth a try."

While Dad's making a green salad, I give Gretchen a quick call. She's in the middle of cooking dinner with her mom, so I explain quickly what I need her to do. To her credit, she doesn't ask a lot of questions—or any, really. "Leave it to me," she says. And I do.

Finally, the pasta's ready. I set the table, and Dad brings the dishes over. The pasta and sauce are steaming when he takes off the lids.

"It smells good," I say.

"I think the ingredients make a difference. I got these vegetables from a little organic market near work. Next year, I'm hoping to grow some in the garden."

"Cool," I say.

We serve ourselves, and I take a bite of the spaghetti cooked just right, and the sauce—a little bit more garlicky than my friends and I usually make it.

"Maybe we could do this for Mom and Kelsie sometime," I say.

"I'd like that," Dad says. "And Emory too. Unless you think that would be too weird."

"I don't know. I guess we'll need to see what happens."

Dad takes a big bite of pasta and chews it thoughtfully. "Do you want me to have a word with your mom? About... what we talked about?"

"No—not yet. Give me a chance to do it first."

Dad agrees. We each have seconds of spaghetti and salad, and then he tries the dessert that Violet and I made. Even though it was easy to make—all we did was mix together strawberries, cream, and little broken-up pieces of meringue—the textures are really good together, and it's light and fresh.

"Delicious," Dad says, after taking a huge bite. He smiles. "I'd like to say you got your cooking talent from me, but I could never do anything like this!"

I laugh. "You might be able to if you check out the recipe on the website. We try to keep things as simple as possible so anyone can make them."

"You mean you'd have me as a member of the Secret Cooking Club?"

I smile proudly. "'The Little Cook' already has thousands of followers," I say. "But between you and me, she's always happy when one more person joins up."

THE SECRET COOKING CLUB

May 6

Guess what? My dad can cook! I said things were kind of weird with me lately, and that's the truth. But one good thing has happened. Recently, my dad came back to live in town. I didn't want to see him at first because I was upset by some things he did in the past—leaving my mom and our family and stuff. But I decided that I'd give him a chance. We got together and cooked a big pot of spaghetti Bolognese and salad. My friend and I made an Eton mess for dessert—it was really easy and quick to make, and tasted really yummy—full of cream and berries, and crunchy meringue. I'm not saying everything is perfect now—far from it. But I'm happy to say that cooking together has brought us closer, and I feel better about him than I have in a long time! I even invited him to join the club. So Dad, if you're reading this...welcome to the Secret Cooking Club.

The Little Cook

xx

CHAPTER 34

A Monster Banished

WHEN DAD DROPS ME HOME (with a container of leftover spaghetti Bolognese), Kelsie's already asleep and Mom's not in her Cave. I put the container in the fridge and go upstairs. In my room, I sit on my bed and text Violet that everything went well, and that the dessert went down great. She texts me back that the core group of friends: her, Gretchen, Alison, Fraser, Naya, Nick—and…Annabel Greene can all make it tomorrow. My heart feels like it's flipping somersaults—but in a good way. I almost feel like this TV thing might be fun. *If*…they let my friends be part of it. *If*…there's even going to be a wedding.

I leave my phone to charge and go down the hall. There's a light on under Mom's door, and the sound of typing. I knock quietly. "Mom?" I say.

The typing stops. There's a long pause.

"What is it?" the reply finally comes.

Taking it as an invitation, I open the door. Mom's sitting on her bed. All around her are bits of glossy paper torn up like confetti. It's then that I realize—it's the wedding file.

"What are you doing?" I ask, feeling an icy chill go through me.

"What does it look like? The wedding's off." She spreads her hands to indicate the carnage.

"No—it can't be!" I rush over to her and try to put my hand on her shoulder. She pulls away.

"Go to your room, Scarlett. There's nothing you can do."

Ignoring her, I plunk down on the bed, sending up a whirlwind of paper.

"I just don't understand," I say. "You and Em-K—you're good together. You…laugh together. He loves you."

"Nonsense! If he loves me, then why did he walk out?"

"He was angry," I say. "You were fighting."

"You shouldn't have been listening. And why do you care, anyway?"

I shake my head, frustrated that I can't get through to her. "I care because I love you. He's good for…all of us."

"You make it sound like it's a nice fairy tale," Moms says.

"And they rode off into the sunset and lived happily ever after. But did they really?" She raises an eyebrow. "You know that he'll never be your dad. Doesn't that count for anything?"

"Is that what this is about? Dad? Dad coming back? Because, he told me he wasn't trying to stir things up. I believe him." I take a breath, suddenly scared. "Unless…"

I open my mouth and then close it again. I can't deny that once or twice I've had little fantasies late at night, where Dad comes groveling back, Mom takes him in, and we're a family again. But in the morning, when I remember my thoughts, I feel sick to my stomach—like I've been to a carnival and eaten way too many sweets. Because in the light of day, I know the difference between fantasy and reality. But I'm not so sure about Mom.

"Unless you're still in love with him…" I choke out the words.

"In love—with your dad!" She looks at me with a mixture of disgust and disbelief.

Then she laughs bitterly, as tears begin to pour from her eyes.

"For all this time, I thought I hated him," she says. "He left, and it hurt so much—it was so humiliating. Having him back here has brought it all back like it was yesterday. I don't hate him now—I've come to realize that. I just feel like I'm on a roller coaster, churning up inside." She shakes her head. "I can't get married again—can't go through that again."

Something loosens inside my chest, as I try to understand what Mom's saying. "You mean, you're scared, Mom?"

"No…I…" She turns away from me and faces the wall. "When Emory walked out the other day, it was as though I'd been waiting for it all along. A 'self-fulfilling prophecy,' they call it. No man is going to stay around here, living in this kind of mess and chaos." She shakes her head. "I was foolish to want to try again."

"Em-K loves you!" I say, my eyes filling with tears. "He didn't walk out the other day because he was leaving us—like…" I take a breath, "…Dad did. Em-K left because he thought you didn't love him. Because his heart was broken." I press my lips together. "It sounded like the TV show meant more to you than he did."

"No… I mean, that can't be right." She turns to me, her face stricken.

"Please, Mom…" I say, "Em-K wants to marry you. I know it. And he isn't like Dad. He's different. And I thought—no, I still think—that deep down, he makes you happy."

"I don't know." She shakes her head. "I thought I was

doing the right thing by trying to patch things up with your dad—be friends, even. He hurt me, and then I tried to get back at him through the blog. I wanted to make things right before I married again. So I could move on from that chapter of our lives."

I nod. "You needed closure," I say.

"Closure." She looks at me with puzzled admiration. "Yes, I suppose that's it. But then I realized that maybe what happened was my fault, and then I…got scared—as you say." Her eyes widen as if she's horrified by the revelation. "And the TV show, and everything else, and now…well…I don't know."

"Then listen to me," I say. "Em-K loves you, and you love him. Things are less…dramatic than with Dad. They're normal." I hesitate. "No—that's not the right word." I take a breath. "They're good. Really good. And if I have to wear a ridiculous, pink, puffy bridesmaid's dress to prove it, then I will."

Mom looks up in alarm. "I thought we decided on lavender."

"Okay, I guess we did."

She leans against me, taking my hand in hers. "When Emory said he wished we'd elope, I was so angry. Because for a second, it sounded like the perfect solution to everything. No stress, no guest list, no awful white dress that makes me look like a cross between a marshmallow and a zombie. I could picture us—just the two of us—plus you and your sister, of course, and maybe a few friends. I'd wear my white linen dress with the blue flowers, and flip-flops. We'd sit around and eat and drink and laugh, and it would be…" she sighs. "But of course, that isn't what I want. Not really."

"Isn't it, Mom?"

"Oh, Scarlett," she says, shaking her head. "What have I done?"

"Nothing that can't be fixed, hopefully." I focus on trying to lend her my newfound strength. I've been brave and faced my issues with Dad. Now, it's her turn to do the right thing.

"Why don't you go downstairs and give Em-K a call?" I say. "I'll come down and make you a cup of hot chocolate, just after I clean up all this paper."

CHAPTER 35

A New Plan

MAYBE IT'S THE HOT CHOCOLATE working its magic, or maybe it's just that Mom's had enough drama for the minute. But either way, she ends up texting Em-K. I read the message before she sends it—almost like she's willing to let me be the mom for now.

Hi—we need to talk. P.S. I'm sorry about the things I said. Love, Claire

I tell her to add a couple of *X*'s and *O*'s after her name, just to let him know that she wants it to be a good talk, not a bad talk. She adds one X and ruffles my hair, morphing back into mom mode. "Thanks, Scarlett," she says. "I think we can get through this. Together."

"We can—and we will." I take the mugs to the sink and rinse them out. I leave her there, sitting at the table waiting for a response to the message. I've done what I can. Now the rest is up to her.

By the time I'm finally back up in my room, it's almost eleven o'clock. I'm completely exhausted, but there's still an awful lot to do before tomorrow. The conversation I had with Mom has given me another idea—totally impossible and a complete nonstarter, but somehow, I can't get it out of my mind.

I call Violet and tell her. She's already half asleep, but she manages to giggle and tell me I've totally lost my mind. In other words, she's on board if I can pull it off. Then I call Dad. He said he knew Producer Poppy, and I'm going to hold him to that.

I speak to him, and he agrees to help me. I wake up Gretchen—she's grumpier than the others, but I'm relieved when she says, "I think it's a good idea. At least it will put an end to things."

An end to things… Is it too much to hope for?

It's almost midnight by the time I've finished planning and texting. As my head is nodding with exhaustion, longing for my pillow, I send one more message—to Em-K. I know there's a thousand things wrong with my plan, but right now, everything hangs in the balance.

CHAPTER 36

Endings and Beginnings

I MUST HAVE SLEPT DESPITE my racing thoughts, because when I wake up, the sky is rosy-pink and a pigeon is cooing from the rafters. For a second, I worry that I've slept late and ruined everything. But when I roll over and check the screen of my phone, I see that it's only six o'clock. I swing out of bed, determined to get an early start for whatever this day will hold.

Tiptoeing into the corridor, I can hear the sound of Mom breathing, deep in sleep. So far so good. She knows I'm due at the TV station and will be gone all day.

Downstairs, I have a quick breakfast of toast and orange juice. I look again at the plastic bags over the door to Rosemary's kitchen and whisper a silent prayer. If today goes well, Mom and Em-K *will* be putting in that door.

And *I'm* going to make sure it happens.

From the other side of the wall, I hear a noise. A rumbling sound like a kettle boiling. I duck through the plastic.

"Hi," I say. "Mind if I join you?"

Em-K is sitting at the long table, his elbows resting on top, his chin in his hands. Behind him, the kettle clicks off but he makes no move to get up. He glances up at me and nods. Treacle is lying on his lap, purring softly.

He's set out a mug with a tea bag in it. I go over and pour boiling water over it. No milk, no sugar. I barely even have to think about it. I bring him the cup and sit down opposite.

"Thanks," he mumbles, but doesn't touch the cup. I have the urge to reach out and take his hand, like I would to Mom, or Violet, or Kelsie—anyone I love who needs me. *Anyone I love.* But Em-K?

Why not?

"Hey," I say, reaching out. It does feel a bit awkward, but I manage to grab his hand and give it a little squeeze, then pull back. He looks at his hand with sadness in his eyes.

"You know," he says. "The first time I came here after my aunt died, I had this vision. There was a family sitting at the table, and they were laughing and happy. The kitchen was warm and cozy, and there was a delicious smell. We were having roast, I think." He pauses, hesitating. "I don't believe in visions. But I do like stories. From the time I was a boy, I believed in 'happily ever after.' Isn't that silly?"

He glances up at me. It sounds like one of those questions that adults ask you, but they don't really expect you to answer.

"I don't know," I say truthfully. "But I do believe there's something special about this kitchen." I pause for a moment, then continue. "Because I had that same 'vision' too. In a dream."

I remember the morning Mom woke me out of a deep sleep. I had felt so warm, so right. Sitting at this table with my family. Em-K was carving the roast at the head of the table. But there was someone else there too.

Dad.

"Really? The same dream?" Em-K finally picks up the cup and takes a sip of his tea.

"Mom loves you," I say. "You just have to get used to the fact that she's not always very good at showing it. Don't stories teach you that nobody's perfect?"

He stares at the dark liquid in his cup without answering.

"In your dream…" He pauses. "Was I…?" He trails off.

"In it?" I give a little smile. "Yeah, you were. I mean— hello!—do you think I'd tell you about it if you weren't?"

"No." He brightens. "I don't."

"Well, then." I keep staring at him until he's forced to look at me. "You need to sort it out—today." I think about how I've had heart-to-hearts with Mom, Dad, and now—Em-K. Sometimes I wonder if all grown-ups are completely ridiculous! To me, things seem so clear.

"I don't know if we can, Scarlett." He hangs his head, looking broken. "No matter what I do—no matter how many times I tell her I love her—she doesn't believe it. And this big wedding has made everything worse. It's just setting things up for failure." He sighs. "And then there's the *other* issue. But really—we probably shouldn't be having this conversation."

"But we are," I say. "And I think I can guess the other issue. It's Dad, isn't it?"

He shrugs. "Like I said—"

"Look, I understand. I thought it was weird too—at first. But believe me, you don't have anything to worry about."

"But he's your dad."

"I know. But she's not in love with him. I know, because I asked her. She wanted to be friends with him—work things out to get closure. But then she started getting scared. That what happened before will happen again. And then she started making it happen. A 'self-fulfilling prophecy.' That's why she's been pushing you away."

Em-K shakes his head. "You're right, Scarlett. This is silly—sitting around, feeling sorry for myself. After all, I'm supposed to be the grown-up here. I shouldn't have said that stuff before—about dreams and visions and happy endings."

"Whoa," I say. "That's not what I meant. I don't think those things are silly at all. I think you can make it happen... *we* can make it happen."

"You mentioned that in your text," Em-K says, frowning. "What exactly did you have in mind?"

And I tell him my plan.

CHAPTER 37

So Much Fun

I'VE DONE WHAT I CAN, and in the end, I have to leave Mom and Em-K to mend their own differences—or not. Whatever happens, I've made a commitment—to my friends, to Mom, to Producer Polly, and to the Secret Cooking Club. It's one I intend to keep.

As Em-K leaves the kitchen—he's agreed, at least, to think about what I've said—he turns back to me. "You're only thirteen," he muses. "But you're so wise. Why is that, Scarlett?"

"I guess I'm simply used to dealing with Mom and her dramas," I say. I hope that this time, I've done enough.

When he's gone, I put extra food in Treacle's dish and slide the special recipe book in my bag. I also gather a few pans and some of the key ingredients together. Even though

Assistant Annie promised me that everything we need to make the wedding feast will be there for us when we arrive, I don't want to leave anything to chance. A car pulls up outside just as Violet arrives at the door. Assistant Annie gets out and greets me cheerfully. If she's nervous about our little "plan," she isn't letting on. She and Violet help me load the car, and just like that we're good to go. Violet and I get in, and she drives away. On the way to the TV station, we stop by to pick up Fraser and Alison. The others are going to meet us there.

"I'm so excited," Alison says, getting into the car. "I've never been on TV before."

My stomach churns with nerves, but I manage to keep smiling. "I'm sure you'll be a natural," I say. "Unlike some of us."

"Don't worry about a thing," says Assistant Annie. "Just act as you would normally. I've ordered in all the ingredients you asked for—they're already at the studio. It will all be so much fun."

I think of all the dishes we're planning to cook—starters, mains, desserts—the entire menu we came up with. I think of the collapsed cake. I think of Mom and Em-K—will they be making up or breaking up? I think of the tension that's still there sometimes between Gretchen and me, and I think of the TV cameras recording every moment of the day that's to come.

I think of the big, over-the-top finale I'm planning—and how a lot of it depends on a man that just a few days ago, I wanted out of my life for good. *Dad.*

"Sure," I say, biting my lip. "So much fun."

CHAPTER 38

Ready, Steady...

IT DOESN'T TAKE LONG TO reach the studio. When we arrive and I get out of the car, I feel like I'm sinking in quicksand. I remember how nervous I felt at the Bridal Center with all the cameras and lights swarming around me. But this is too important—I can't back out now. I clutch the bag with *The Little Cook* to my chest, hoping that just for today, our special book will continue to work is magic.

Gretchen, Nick, Naya, and Annabel Greene are waiting in the lobby of the studios when we arrive.

"Hello!" I say to Annabel, giving her a quick hug. Her face is very pale, and I can tell that she's just as nervous as I am—and probably a lot more so. "I'm so glad you're here! I've told everyone about your fantastic cupcakes."

"Thanks," she says. "I was kind of scared to come, to be honest. I mean, you guys are such great cooks, and great friends, and…"

"And we're delighted to have you," Violet chips in.

I introduce the others. "But don't worry if you can't remember everyone's name," I reassure her.

"Yeah," Gretchen says. "This is a new thing for all of us."

"Thanks," Annabel says, a little color returning to her cheeks.

"No worries," I say. "Today of all days, we need all the help we can get."

The eight of us gather the things from the car to carry inside. Just as Assistant Annie is about to direct us to the studio, a woman in a red dress and high heels swoops down on us. It's Producer Poppy.

"Scarlett!" She presses my cheeks together and gives me an air kiss. "How delightful to see you and…" She looks around me and frowns. "Your friends."

I take a breath through my teeth. "I know we didn't discuss it, but I can't appear on your show by myself to do the wedding cake." My knees feel like jelly as I speak, but I force myself to keep my chin up and my voice strong. "I'm the founder of the Secret Cooking Club. And that means, if I'm going to cook on your show, then so are they. We're here to do a whole wedding feast."

"Right." Producer Poppy puts her hands on her hips and stares at me. I stare back, gaining strength from my having my friends around me. "I need a word with my assistant." They move just out of earshot and seem to be having a heated discussion.

"What's happening?" Annabel asks.

"You didn't have to do that," Gretchen whispers to me.

I smile at both of them, hoping I look more confident than I feel. "Yes, I did," I say. "Because it's absolutely true."

"And you think they'll go for it?" Gretchen raises an eyebrow.

"I don't—"

At that moment, the lobby door opens again and a man enters. Tall, broad-shouldered, darkish blond hair. *Dad.*

"Poppy!" He shows his pass to the guard and swoops up, giving her a quick peck on the cheek. "I see they're all here, just like I said they would be! This is going to be fabulous for your show and the ratings."

Immediately, Producer Poppy seems to melt. And at that moment, I know for absolutely certain: Dad isn't a risk to our future happiness—not where Mom's concerned, anyhow. He's already seeing someone else.

"Well, yes," she stammers, "I hope so."

He takes Poppy to the side and speaks to her in a low voice. I know he's telling her about the rest of my "plan." Her eyebrows rise and fall, and she glances over at me a few times, looking worried. She shakes her head, and for a second, I worry that it's all gone wrong. Then, she smiles.

"Okay," she says, loud enough for us all to hear it. "I'll let the crew know about the...um..." she clears her throat, "... slight change in plan."

Dad gives me a thumbs-up and presses the button for the elevator. "Hope you kids have a great time," he says. "I'm off to take Kelsie to get a new scooter, but I'll be on my cell if you need me."

"Great." I grin. "Thanks."

"Who's that?" Annabel asks as soon as he's gone.

"My dad." I smile proudly.

My friends and I follow Assistant Annie out of the lobby and down a corridor that ends in a large door. The door leads to another corridor, and eventually she stops in front of a door marked STUDIO 5. "This is it," Annie says.

Halfway inside, I stop so suddenly that Violet pushes into my back. "Oh my gosh!" I say, amazed at what's before me.

There are more gasps, oohs and ahs from behind me as the Secret Cooking Club members file in to our kitchen-for-the-day. It's a huge space—almost twice the size of Rosemary's kitchen—and even bigger than our school cafeteria kitchen! Every surface is white and shiny, sparkling and spotless. Even the floor is white, polished like an ice rink. The floor is raised up a little, almost like a stage. In front of the raised part and immediately around where we're standing, is a forest of cameras, microphones, lights, and wires.

"Um, where should we put this stuff?" Nick says. He and Fraser have come in behind the rest of us, their arms full of the pans and books I've brought.

"Put it on the far counter." Assistant Annie points to the edge of the kitchen where there are almost a dozen giant carrier bags full of the ingredients we asked for. "That will be out of shot."

Violet and I look at each other as we walk toward the raised floor. My legs are wobbly, but I make myself keep going. I step up on to the gleaming white floor. Violet comes up too, and the others follow.

"Okay," I say, "this is where we'll be cooking today. Obviously." My voice sounds small in the large space. I gesture to Gretchen, who nods. She takes out the menus and the photocopied recipes. Opening my bag, I take out *The Little Cook*. I'm glad to see there's a book stand in the kitchen, and I prop it open. Seeing it there, I feel a little less on edge.

Producer Poppy comes back into the room, looking harried. A man is following behind her—they look like they've been arguing.

She claps her hands to get everyone's attention. "Well," she says, smoothing her skirt, "we weren't really expecting a... club. But we're going to go with it." Her smile has that stressed look I'm used to seeing from Mom, only with lipstick.

"I'll need the phone numbers of all your parents," the man says. "I'll need to get some waivers and permissions signed. But no reason to hold up the show." His smile seems genuine.

"Great," I say. My heart feels like it's just run a fifty-yard dash. "We'll get set up."

It doesn't take me long to figure out that my friends are all as nervous as I am, even Gretchen—and as the PTA rep for our year, she's used to speaking with grown-ups. Everyone talks in whispers. The cameramen come in, and the producer talks to them individually and introduces us to a short, balding man who's the director. Then a woman comes around to me with a little box that clips on to the waistband of my jeans, and a cord that comes around and clips on to the front of my apron—a microphone, she says. Even though I've spoken into microphones before when doing charity bake-offs, having one clipped on to me makes my heart gallop. What if I breathe too loudly or, without thinking, accidently mutter a rude word? The woman has three more microphones. I direct her to clip them on Nick, Alison, and Gretchen. The others: Fraser, Violet, Annabel, and Naya all look relieved not to have a mic. Another woman hovers around with a palette of makeup and a hairbrush. Alison goes over to have a chat and ends up taking a brush herself to help apply powder to each of our faces.

Finally, Producer Poppy comes back over. "Okay, here's how this is going to work." She goes on to explain the cameras, and the microphones, and how the cameras are going to move around to get different angles. Then she tells us to "just look natural."

As if!

She rushes off to speak to the cameramen, and I hold up my hand to gather all my friends together.

"Thanks for coming," I say. The microphone amplifies my voice, but I ignore it. "We've been through the plan and everybody knows what they're supposed to be doing, right?"

Heads nod, still nervous.

"It's all there on the sheet I did," Gretchen says. She and Naya have already handed around a schedule of who's doing what. "Now, if you have any questions, come and see me or Scarlett, okay?"

"Yeah." I smile. Now that Gretchen's in charge, she seems much more at ease. "And the most important thing—the reason we're all here—is because this is what we love. So let's get started, and have some fun."

It may sound a little silly, but I raise my hand in a high-five. Everyone else puts their hands in the middle too, just like we might have done when we were little kids. The energy begins to flow between us, and all of a sudden, worried faces turn to smiles.

"Ready…" I say.

"Steady…" everyone joins in.

"Bake!"

· CHAPTER 39 ·

Confetti and Cakes

I LOSE MYSELF...

In the feel of the flour as it thickens when I stir it in the bowl, the butter and sugar mixing together. In the smell of the lemon peel, the fresh fruit, the caramel. In the laughter, the occasional floury hand on my shoulder, in the bright lights and the white surface that is no longer shiny, but covered with sugar and pastry ends, gravy, doughy spoons, vegetable peelings, and eggshells. In the moment when I put each cake tier, one by one, into the shiny steel oven to bake, and the moment when I open the door and the sweet-smelling steam rushes up to warm my face. And the cameras don't matter, or the microphones, or the directions spoken by the producer.

One by one, canapé by canapé, dish by dish, layer by layer, the wedding feast gets made. Violet and Annabel oversee the desserts and help me decorate the cake, Gretchen and Nick focus on the mains, Fraser and Naya on the starters. Alison pitches in where necessary, peeling the fruit, and making the sparkling lemonade and miniature milkshakes. She ends up doing quite a bit of speaking in front of the camera, explaining what we're all doing. Maybe because it's because she's so pretty, but she's a natural on the screen.

As I make each tier of the cake, I tick off the ingredients as I put them in to avoid another baking powder disaster. Violet makes new "bride and groom" figures for the top of the cake out of sugar paste. Hers don't look a lot more like Mom and Em-K than mine did, if I'm honest, but they are more artistic, and the silver and white edible glitter on the dress does look lovely. But as the cake nears completion, my nerves rise to the surface. Because as much as the wedding feast prepared by the Secret Cooking Club seems to be a success, on camera at least, I need the other part—the most important part—of my plan to come together too. I wipe a layer of flour off my watch and check the time. It's almost three o'clock. If something's going to happen, it will have to be soon.

Just then, I hear a high-pitched voice as a small figure dashes into the studio. Producer Poppy looks alarmed. "Who's that child?" she says.

Kelsie runs up on to the stage. "Oooh, look at that cake," she says. "It looks so fab-u-licious!"

I take a step back and look at what Violet and Annabel have done. The six tiers of the cake are covered with smooth white icing. Violet has piped on an intricate white border of buttercream around each tier, and she and Annabel have used royal icing and edible glue to paste real flowers covered in glitter—rose petals, crystallized violets, pansies, and lavender florets—all down the side of the cake like a magic swirl.

Kelsie squeezes my hand. "Dad and I did what you said, Scarlett," she says. "He talked to her in the kitchen, and I went upstairs to her room and got the dress and flip-flops. And your purple T-shirt."

"Great job," I say. She hands it to me and I slip it over the white one I'm wearing. "But just for today, the T-shirt's *lavender*, okay?"

"Yeah!"

"Kelsie!" My sister and I both turn. It's Mom.

She looks beyond stressed, but at least her hair is wet, which means she's showered. Producer Poppy immediately waylays her. Naya puts Kelsie to work helping to finish the canapés, and I strain to hear what Poppy and Mom are talking about.

"Makeup? Why do you want me in makeup?" Mom says.

"We thought it might be good to get some footage of you with your daughters while they're baking," Poppy says. "We'll put you in a nice dress, and it will be brilliant. So good for the show."

"Well, if you think it will be good for the show…" Mom brightens.

"Yes. So if you'll just go with my assistant, she'll take you down to your own dressing room…"

"Did Mom talk to Em-K?" I whisper to my sister.

"I…" Her blue eyes widen. "I…don't know. They are going to get married, right?" There's a hesitation in her voice. "That's what Dad says."

"Did he? Did you get your scooter?"

"Yes!" She grins. "It's totally awesome. It's pink."

"Good."

Her smile fades. "Dad says that Em-K can help me ride it. That he's going to be our new stepdad."

"And are you okay with that?" My jaw tenses as I wait for her answer.

"I guess so. Dad says that we're lucky because we'll have two dads. We'll get twice as many presents."

I laugh, ruffling her blond hair. "With two dads, I guess we will."

All the ingredients are in place, separate things ready to be mixed together into something new—like they belonged that way all along. The wedding feast, The Secret Cooking Club, even the TV cameras. Violet's hand is perfectly steady as she positions the little sugar-paste bride figure on top of the cake. But there's one piece of the puzzle that's still missing.

I go to the side of the stage where the cameras can't see me and check my phone to see if there's been any response to the texts I've sent. Texts to the one person who can make or break this now. There's no response. I feel a chilling sensation running down my spine. In front of three cameras, Violet sets the figure of the groom on top of the cake next to the bride. Will all this be for nothing?

The studio door opens. A few women come in whom I recognize as friends of Mom. There are only four of them, but I figure it's not bad for only a few hours' notice. Behind them, an elderly man in a dark suit and white collar enters.

Producer Poppy rushes up to the newcomers. "How fantastic you could all make it at such short notice!" Even though she's been on her feet in those high heels for eight hours, there's no sign of her flagging. She looks around and frowns. "Let me take you to the studio next door. That's where we're hoping to start filming in…" she checks her watch, "…ten minutes. All being well."

But all is not well. Mom comes into the studio, followed by a breathless Assistant Annie who has obviously been told to keep her as far away from the cameras as possible. Mom's wearing her flowered dress, but not her flip-flops. Those are in Annie's hand.

"Will someone tell me what's going on?" Mom says. "Why I'm—oh!"

She spies the cake and her mouth drops open. Then, she looks around at the feast we've laid out on a table at the edge of the white kitchen counters. A feast we made in part for the benefit of the cameras, but in the end, I swear—that each dish, every canapé, each dollop of icing, and sparkly edible flower was made with love. It's a feast fit for a bride and groom; a feast fit for a new family. If only—

The studio door opens again. I feel shaky with nerves as Dad walks in, tall and straight in a pair of tan trousers and a blue shirt. And behind him is another man—shorter, but with every inch the same authority. He's wearing a black suit and a white shirt, but his tie is loose around his neck.

Dad steps back, standing next to Producer Poppy. I notice him reach out and brush her hand. But that's all I notice about them, because all eyes are drawn to the other man. Congressman Emory Kruffs. Down on one knee. And Mom, kicking off her shoes, running over to him.

"Camera one!" someone whispers.

"Claire," Em-K says, his voice hoarse with emotion. "A little bird told me that in your heart of hearts, you still want to marry me. That you had some things to come to terms with, and then there was the stress of the wedding. And I guess that if I'm honest, I was kind of scared too. But at the end of the day, I want to be with you. Forever."

"I...I..." Mom stammers. I don't remember her ever being speechless before, but I guess there's a first time for everything.

"That little bird also told me that you might be open to doing something really outrageous—like eloping. Getting married on a beach, in a summer dress and flip-flops."

The flip-flops materialize from Annie's hand at Mom's feet. She steps into them.

"And, of course, with the most beautiful wedding feast

anyone could ever imagine." Em-K's smile seems to light up the whole room. He takes Mom's hand, and the glowing bubble extends around her as well.

"So maybe I haven't exactly got a beach, but I can tell you that in the studio next door, there's some sand and a nice sunny backdrop. There's also a vicar and some of your best friends."

Tears flow down Mom's face, but fortunately, it seems the makeup lady used waterproof mascara.

"So, I know this is kind of short notice, but, Claire, will you run away with me? Elope? It will just be us, the children, a few friends, the Secret Cooking Club…and a national TV audience."

"Oh, Emory! How fabulous!"

They start to kiss, and things go kind of blurry as my own eyes fill with tears. Emory leads her off to the side. Mom's crying and gripping his hand, and they're talking to each other—the most important thing of all, I think.

The stage crew comes in and rearranges the walls so the kitchen studio and the soundstage next door are made into one big open space. Dad stands at the back while Producer Poppy and Assistant Annie get on with the million tasks of sorting out lighting and camera angles, and the wedding cake is moved forward into the shot; the vicar says a few words, and my friends and I all gather around. "Quick, get the champagne and canapés ready!" I direct. Gretchen and Naya take charge and make sure the food gets moved to the right place.

I feel wobbly on my feet and overcome with emotion. Everyone is busy, and no one seems to notice as I slip out of the back door of the studio to the hallway to catch my breath. I lean against the wall, feeling happy and scared and bubbly with adrenaline. The door opens again, and Nick comes out. It hardly seems possible, but my heart speeds up even faster.

"You okay, Scarlett?" he says. "It's all happening, isn't it?"

I look at him for a long second—his wavy brown hair, almond-shaped brown eyes, the face that launched a thousand crushes, now etched with concern—for me. And then I start to laugh. Great gulping laughter that makes it hard to breathe and shakes my whole body. The concern on his face turns to alarm, and then, a second later, he's laughing too. And then almost before I realize it, he's put his arms around me, and he's stopped laughing. His hair falls over his eyes and he pushes it back nervously. And then, he brushes his lips against mine. And I stop laughing, lift my chin and press my lips to his. I try to relax and then start enjoying it—my first real kiss!

And I'm not even embarrassed when the studio door opens again and Assistant Annie sticks her head out and announces that everything's ready—well, not too embarrassed anyway.

Nick and I slowly come apart, and my head feels as if it's shimmering like light on water.

"So I guess you *are* my girlfriend." Nick laughs breathlessly (and I can't believe he can even talk at all).

"I guess so," I squeak. I allow him to lead me by the hand back inside the studio. My friends are standing around the stage in a group. I can't stop grinning, and I'm sure that what's happened is written all over my face. But most of them don't even seem to notice that Nick and I have just returned. Only Violet comes up next to me, giving me a sly smile. "There you are," she whispers. "We thought you'd been 'bridesmaid-napped.'"

My whole face is glowing as I smile back at her. "Something like that."

One of the stagehands comes around and passes us each a small plastic bag filled with confetti—tiny bows and hearts made of silver and white paper. The producer gives a signal to the cameraman.

I stand in between Kelsie and Violet as we all join hands, and Mom scrunches her toes in the sand, her face shining with the love—and drama—of it all. And she and Em-K say their vows, and then are pronounced "husband and wife." They kiss each other in a way that makes me blush to the roots of my hair, and hyperaware of Nick standing behind me. And when the happy couple turns to face us, we all cheer and whoop and throw clouds of confetti, showering them with shimmering bows and hearts and good wishes. I feel so happy and full of hope for the future—both my family's and my own. I turn my head slightly to smile at Nick, still feeling flushed at the memory of the kiss. And as I'm turning back, I notice Dad slip out of the back of the studio, his eyes downcast. And I feel a little sad too.

"Scarlett?"

I turn back. Mom's holding out her hand for me to join her. Swallowing hard, I push my nerves aside and go and join her and Em-K and Kelsie on the "beach." The four of us hug each other—so tightly that it takes my breath away. A tear rolls down my cheek, and Mom brushes it off with her finger and kisses me on the forehead. "You even wore lavender for me," she says, beaming.

"I tried—this was the best I could do."

"Thank you so much," she says, "for all of this."

I just hug her more tightly. The spotlights are on us, and the cameras, and I think about how the wedding may not have been exactly what Mom planned, but is definitely something she'll talk about and remember forever. I see the love that's crinkled into Em-K's serious-looking brow, and I feel the joy and the pride as all my friends start talking at once and go over to start serving the food. And I know that it's okay to feel happy and sad, because this moment marks both the end of something, and a new beginning—not just for them, but for *us*.

As I go over to rejoin my friends and help with the food and the cake, the lights pan over me, warm and bright like the morning sun. Violet waves me over to help her pass out the plates for the cake. As I join her, she takes my hand and squeezes it tightly. "You did it, Scarlett," she whispers. "It's wonderful."

"*We* did it," I whisper back with a grin. "And yeah, it really is."

CHAPTER 40

Epilogue

TWO DAYS AFTER THE WEDDING, the door goes in.

Em-K and Mom have both taken the week off, and they've arranged to move their honeymoon forward because, of course, the wedding was sooner than anyone expected. While they're away, Kelsie's going to stay with Dad at his apartment, and I'm going to stay with Violet. But even though everything has changed, for a few days at least, things are almost the same as they were.

For one thing, Kelsie and I still have school. When I go down to the kitchen in the morning, Em-K is there, making coffee for Mom, who's sleeping in. It isn't even that weird to see him there, wearing a bathrobe that Mom gave him for Valentine's Day, over a T-shirt and pajama bottoms.

Okay, to be honest, it is a little weird.

As the coffee burbles away in the machine, I try to act normal. Treacle rubs against my leg, and I reach to pat him. I make some toast and pour myself a glass of orange juice. Em-K gets out a tray to bring Mom breakfast, and as we're both trying not to get into each other's way (without seeming that we're avoiding each other) I end up bumping right into him, the cat squawking underfoot.

"Okay then!" he says. We both start laughing.

"Why don't you let me make breakfast?" I offer. "I've got a little extra time."

"Actually," he says, "why don't you have a seat? I was just about to make some eggs."

"Are you sure?"

He reaches out and takes my arms. A smile lights up his face. "It's the least I can do, Scarlett. To say thank you for what you did. You've made me the happiest man alive."

"Whoa!" I say. "Shouldn't you be saying that to Mom?"

His face goes pink. "Was it very awful?"

"Terrible!"

We both start laughing again.

There are footsteps overhead and then on the stairs. A moment later, Kelsie comes into the kitchen, followed by Mom.

"Everything okay?" Mom asks. Her eyes are shiny, and

her skin, usually dull and pasty in the morning, seems to glow. She looks happy.

I look at Em-K. His smile stretches from ear to ear. He looks at me and winks.

"Things are great," I say. "You two sit down, and Em-K and I will finish making breakfast."

"Okay," she says. She and Kelsie both sit, and I set the table for four—or try to. There's a pile of bills and papers taking up one whole place, and the table is small for four people anyway.

"This is cozy," Em-K says, as he serves the eggs and buttered toast and I pour everyone glasses of orange juice. His eyes flick over to the jagged hole in the wall. "Maybe you could give me the number of the builder later on, Claire," he says. "Unless you want to call."

"Oh, that." Mom waves a hand lazily. Her sparkly engagement ring catches the light, next to the thin platinum band that Em-K put on her finger during the wedding. "You go ahead."

"And are we knocking out the whole wall or putting in a door?"

For a moment, a spark of panic shoots up my spine. An awful lot has happened in the last forty-eight hours, and while we're all still running on adrenaline, it's going to take a while to adjust, surely...

Mom reaches over and puts her hand on top of mine. "Just a door, I think. Assuming that's okay with everyone."

I smile at her, feeling a rush of love. "Thanks," I mouth so softly that no one hears it but her.

THE SECRET COOKING CLUB

June 9

Lemon and Lavender Cake

- 3 cups all-purpose flour
- 1 tablespoon baking powder
- ¼ teaspoon salt
- 1 tablespoon dried edible lavender
- 1 cup butter, softened
- 1½ cups sugar
- 4 tablespoons lemon zest
- 4 eggs
- ¾ cup Greek yogurt

Preheat the oven to 350 degrees. Lightly grease and flour two 7-inch round cake pans, and set aside. Combine flour, baking powder, salt, and lavender in a medium bowl. Set aside. In a separate large bowl, beat the butter and sugar until light and fluffy. Add the lemon zest and eggs to the butter mixture, one egg at a time, incorporating each egg completely before adding the next. Add Greek yogurt into wet ingredients and mix. Fold dry ingredients into the wet ingredients until combined. Divide mixture evenly into the greased cake pans. Bake for 45 to 50 minutes, or until inserted toothpick comes out clean. Let cakes cool completely on wire racks, then decorate with the frosting and toppings of your choice!

Okay, so I'm kind of scared to mention this, but tonight's the night. *Wedding Belles*: Episode Five, "Confetti and Cake" is premiering on Channel 3 at eight o'clock. They asked me if I wanted to watch it in advance, but I said no. I've got some friends coming over, and we'll sit around and watch it together. My dad's coming over too. He's going to cook up a big pot of spaghetti for everyone, and the rest of us are doing garlic bread, salad, and tiramisu for dessert. But right now, I feel so nervous, I don't know how I can possibly eat.

I guess in the end, it doesn't matter whether I

look silly, or like a deer in the headlights in front of the camera. The main thing is that we made a lovely wedding feast for my mom and Em-K, and that one month later, things are going pretty well. It's not even weird. Okay, maybe a little weird—but I'll get there.

Before the whole wedding thing even started, I wished I had a recipe for dealing with all the changes in my life. But the last few months have taught me that as long as I'm using the best ingredients— friends, family, love, truth, and self-confidence—then no matter what happens, I can handle it.

So tonight, all I can do is be brave. (And keep hold of the remote in case I need to turn the TV off in a hurry!)

The Little Cook

xx

I hit post and run downstairs just as the doorbell rings. Dad's already in the kitchen making a huge pot of spaghetti, so it must be someone else, arriving early. Or maybe it's Mom and Em-K—they went out to the store to pick up a few last-minute things. And we'll all be having dinner together, just like in the dream I had that now seems a lifetime ago. But they wouldn't have rung the doorbell…

I go to the door and fling it open.

"Surprise!" My heart jolts from the sound—they're all here! All my friends, and "costars" of tonight's show: Nick and Violet, Fraser and Naya, Gretchen and Alison, Annabel Greene…standing outside the door, each carrying something in their arms. Cupcakes, loaves of bread, salad, a big pink bowl of popcorn. I grin from ear to ear and feel the nerves and excitement course through my body. This, after all, is *our* night.

"We thought we'd come early to help with dinner," Naya says.

"And bring some extra food in case we want to watch the show more than once." Nick leans in and gives me a kiss on cheek.

"Come in!" I stand aside, my knees a little bit wobbly. "I'm so glad you're here!"

I usher them into the front room, and everyone sits on

the extra chairs and beanbags that Kelsie and I have set out. Fraser and Nick run to the kitchen to get some more plates and bowls. And the rest of us chat and pass around the popcorn, and trickle into the kitchen to help.

A while later, when everything's ready, we all sit around the table. Mom is at one end, with Em-K at the other. Dad and I are across from each other in the middle. Everyone else is filling in the gaps on either side. There's an energy in the room as everyone talks and laughs, and Nick and Fraser carry the TV into the room. Treacle is beside himself, jumping from lap to lap and purring, in heaven from so many people to give him attention.

The food is delicious, and even though I'm nervous, I still manage to eat a helping and a half. And a few minutes before eight, I tap my spoon on the edge of my glass of orange juice, and gradually the room falls silent.

This time, even though everyone's looking at me, I don't feel my normal stage fright—not too much, anyway. "I'd like to propose a toast," I say. "To friends, old and new." My eyes sweep down the table, pausing on the face of each and every person here—the people I love. "And, of course," I add, "to the Secret Cooking Club!"

"To friends!"

"To the Secret Cooking Club!" Everyone is chorusing and clinking glasses.

"To the bride and groom!" Dad adds, lifting his glass.

"To my two dads!" Kelsie yells out.

"*Two* minutes to eight," Nick says. From his place at the table next to Dad, he hands me the remote control.

"It's time, Scarlett," he says.

It's time.

Violet jumps out of her chair and runs over to the light switch. "Is everybody ready?" She dims the lights to a low amber.

"As ready as I'll ever be." I point the remote and switch on the television.

Acknowledgments

I'd like to say thank you to all the young readers out there who love cooking and baking—you are the continuing inspiration behind the Secret Cooking Club books. This year, I've had the privilege to meet and talk to some of you at school events, and I've enjoyed every moment and learned so much! I'd also like to thank the teachers, parents, and librarians who have also given me encouragement to write this book, and the staff at St. Hilary's School who let me be a judge for their real-life charity bake-off. Next, I'd like to mention the people at Chicken House who are true champions of new writers and have been so helpful and supportive to me in building my career as an author. Also, thanks to my agent, Anna Power, and my writing group—Ronan Winters, Chris King, Francisco Gochez, David Speakman, and Lucy Beresford, who have helped me to remain positive during some of the challenges I've faced this year.

And most of all, I'd like to thank my family—my parents,

Suzanne and Bruce, Monica Yeo, my partner, Ian, and especially my three lovely daughters: Eve, Rose, and Grace. You give meaning to my life and make it all worthwhile.

About the Author

Laurel Remington works as a lawyer for a renewable energy company that builds wind farms. She lives in the UK with her three girls.

FIND OUT HOW SCARLETT'S BAKING
ADVENTURE BEGAN IN...

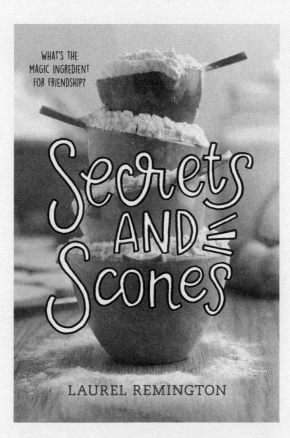

"As heartwarming as a fresh
cinnamon scone."

—*Kirkus Reviews*